FATAL FLIP

PEG MARBERG

BERKLEY PRIME CRIME, NEW YORK

THE BERKLEY PUBLISHING GROUP
Published by the Penguin Group
Penguin Group (USA) Inc.
375 Hudson Street, New York, New York 10014, USA
Penguin Group (Canada), 90 Eglinton Avenue East, Suite 700, Toronto, Ontario M4P 2Y3, Canada
(a division of Pearson Penguin Canada Inc.)
Penguin Books Ltd., 80 Strand, London WC2R 0RL, England
Penguin Group Ireland, 25 St. Stephen's Green, Dublin 2, Ireland (a division of Penguin Books Ltd.)
Penguin Group (Australia), 250 Camberwell Road, Camberwell, Victoria 3124, Australia
(a division of Pearson Australia Group Pty. Ltd.)
Penguin Books India Pvt. Ltd., 11 Community Centre, Panchsheel Park, New Delhi—110 017, India
Penguin Group (NZ), 67 Apollo Drive, Rosedale, North Shore 0632, New Zealand
(a division of Pearson New Zealand Ltd.)
Penguin Books (South Africa) (Pty.) Ltd., 24 Sturdee Avenue, Rosebank, Johannesburg 2196,
South Africa

Penguin Books Ltd., Registered Offices: 80 Strand, London WC2R 0RL, England

This is a work of fiction. Names, characters, places, and incidents either are the product of the author's
imagination or are used fictitiously, and any resemblance to actual persons, living or dead, business
establishments, events, or locales is entirely coincidental. The publisher does not have any control
over and does not assume any responsibility for author or third-party websites or their content.

FATAL FLIP

A Berkley Prime Crime Book / published by arrangement with the author

PRINTING HISTORY
Berkley Prime Crime mass-market edition / March 2009

Copyright © 2009 by Peg Marberg.
Cover illustration by Mary Ann Lasher.
Interior text design by Laura K. Corless.

ISBN: 978-0-425-22679-7

BERKLEY® PRIME CRIME
Berkley Prime Crime Books are published by The Berkley Publishing Group,
a division of Penguin Group (USA) Inc.,
375 Hudson Street, New York, New York 10014.
BERKLEY® PRIME CRIME and the PRIME CRIME logo are trademarks of Penguin Group
(USA) Inc.

PRINTED IN THE UNITED STATES OF AMERICA

10   9   8   7   6   5   4   3   2   1

This book is dedicated to all my family,
Eddie and Deb, Rich and Lisa,
Ann-Margret and Mike,
with a special tip of the hat to
my son-in-law Mike Rzyski,
who pointed me in the right direction
when I was floundering. Thanks, Mike.

ACKNOWLEDGMENTS

As I've said before but it's so important
that I'll say it again—I could not have written
this book without the aid of two people—
my husband, Ed, and my editor, Sandra Harding.
They are always there when I need them.
Thank you both from the bottom
of my heart and my inkwell.

CITIZENS OF
SEVILLE, INDIANA

Jean Hastings	------	Interior designer and amateur sleuth
Charlie Hastings	------	Jean's husband and retired investment counselor
JR Cusak	------	The Hastings' married daughter and Jean's business partner
Matt Cusak	------	JR's husband and police lieutenant
Kerry, Kelly, and Kris Cusak	------	JR and Matt's children
Mary England	------	Charlie's twin sister and Jean's best friend
Denny England	------	Mary's husband and owner of England's Fine Furniture

Amanda Little	------	Real estate agent
Sid Rosen, Patti Crump, and Jasper Merkle	------	Seville police officers
Horatio Bordeaux	------	Entrepreneur and Jean's friend
Mrs. Daggert	------	Horatio's housekeeper
Biddy McFarland	------	Seville's top gossip
Vilma Beatty	------	Biddy's elderly mother
Ben Kind	------	President and owner of B. Kind Sure Mortgage Company
Duke Demarco	------	General contractor
Herbie Waddlemeyer	------	Employee of England's Fine Furniture
Arthur Kraft	------	Local florist

VISITORS TO
SEVILLE, INDIANA

Stuart Goodenough ------ Real estate broker

Harry Eastwood ------ Retired plastic manufacturer

Bambi Eastwood ------ Harry's young wife and former exotic dancer

Harriet Eastwood ------ Harry's grown daughter

Danny Semple ------ Popular heavy metal rocker and rising star, stage name Danny Danger

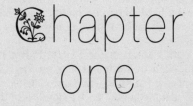Chapter
one

❧

Biddy McFarland peeked through the lace panels covering the side parlor's curved, ceiling-to-floor windows that provided her with an excellent view of the house next door. The house was owned and occupied by Edith Semple, an elderly spinster. The Semple manse, like the McFarland manse, was Victorian in style and constructed during the 1890s building boom that occurred in our small central Indiana town of Seville.

Almost all the houses in Seville, regardless of age, have been the recipients of tender, loving care with very few exceptions, the most glaring one being the Semple manse. The crumbling old Victorian looked like something out of an early Hollywood horror flick.

Hidden from the street by a tangle of overgrown shrubbery, the decrepit structure, along with its reclusive owner, became a true case of out of sight, out of mind. And that's pretty much how it remained for everyone but Biddy McFarland, who took it as her neighborly duty to spy on old Edith. Thanks to Biddy's unflagging devotion to "duty," the foul odor emitting from the Semple house was promptly reported to the police, who arrived to find a rather ghastly scene. Edith Semple had passed on.

From the comfort of her charming, updated Victorian, Biddy watched the comings and goings of the police and the medical personnel as they dealt with death and its aftermath. For Biddy McFarland, a middle-aged, happy homemaker and Seville's foremost gossip, it would be an evening to remember.

"Officer Patti Crump of the Seville Police Department discovered the body of Edith Semple after Mrs. Gordon McFarland, a concerned neighbor, reported a terrible stench emitting from the Semple home," I read aloud from the morning edition of the *Sentinel*'s front page while my husband, Charlie, was polishing off a quick breakfast of sourdough toast and coffee. My own breakfast remained untouched as I waited for his comment.

A dedicated golfer, Charlie wasn't about to allow the news of Edith Semple's passing to interfere with his early tee time at the Sleepy Hollow Country Club's eighteen-hole golf course on such a lovely summer day.

"Well, I guess that's that," said Charlie, depositing what was left of his toast into the open mouth of Pesty, our pampered, overweight Keeshond. The dog is a canine garbage disposal.

" 'That's that'? What kind of a response is that?" I demanded, adding, "Charles William Hastings, either you're the most uncaring person in the world or you haven't heard a single word I've said." After more than thirty-five years of marriage to the man, my money was on the latter.

"Sweetheart, you know that's not true. I heard every word you said. I only meant that since Edith lived to be ninety-eight and the police are treating the matter as a death from natural causes, that pretty well wraps things up. The old gal died the way she lived. All alone without any family or friends. That was her choice. End of story. Especially as far as you're concerned."

A successful investment counselor, Charlie took an early retirement some twelve-plus years ago. It came at a time when I was struggling with empty-nest syndrome caused by the marriage of our only child, Jean junior (aka JR), to her college sweetheart, Matthew Cusak. In an effort to keep my sanity, I returned to college, earned a degree, passed the National Council for Interior Design exam, and joined the United Federation of Interior Designers (UFID). Not long after that, I established the firm of Designer Jeans with my daughter, JR, as my junior partner.

Along with a talent for solving design and decorating dilemmas, I seemed to have developed a talent for crime solving, something that drives both Charlie and our son-in-law Matt (a Seville police lieutenant) a bit nuts. I didn't need Charlie's comment regarding Seville's finest handling the Semple matter to remind me that I'm a designer and not a detective. But it didn't stop me from challenging Charlie's account of Edith's passing.

"Show me where in the article the authorities say the death was from natural causes, chum," I snapped, pushing the newspaper over to where Charlie was sitting at the round, oak table.

"Oh, for chrissake, Jean, I haven't got time to go into that right now." As if on cue, the sound of an automobile horn bounced through the open top of the kitchen's Dutch door.

"Hey, that's Denny," Charlie announced, referring to Dennis England, his brother-in-law, owner of England's Fine Furniture, and golf partner. "Sorry, kid, I've got to go."

A quick kiss to my cheek along with a fast pat to the top of Pesty's fuzzy head, and my silver-haired, blue-eyed, perpetually tan Prince Charming was off and running.

"I love you, too," I hollered to the fast-retreating figure, "and don't forget we're having dinner with Mary"— Charlie's twin sister and my lifelong, very best friend— "and Denny tonight." I would have mentioned the time and place (six thirty in the main dining room of the country club) but the sound of Denny's ancient MG's motor drowned out everything, including Charlie's reply.

Pouring myself a second cup of coffee, I lit a cigarette and settled down for a more careful reading of Hilly Murrow's article. Charlie was right about the police handling the matter as a routine, natural death. I must have missed that part the first time around because of Hilly's propensity to exaggerate even the most mundane news. Most of what she'd reported was a rehash of the sad saga of the Semple family and the sorry state of the house and Edith herself.

Like everyone else in town I, Jean Hastings—wife, mother, grandmother, and interior designer—knew the sorry tale of the Semple family by heart. In 1896, Henry Semple, the wealthy manufacturer of Semple's Seafaring Steamer Trunks, purchased the house as a gift for his bride, Edna Mae. The Semples were well into their forties when Edith, their only child, was born.

In 1933, both Edna Mae and Henry were diagnosed with tuberculosis. Henry supposedly convinced his wife that suicide was a cheaper alternative to an illness that could be as expensive as it was lengthy. Edith, who by then was an adult, had assumed the role of unpaid housekeeper for her parents. It was she who discovered the couple hanging side by side in the cellar amongst jars of preserved fruits, vegetables, and pickled pigs' feet.

Edith's life seemed to finally be headed in a brighter direction when shortly after the loss of her parents, she fell in love with Calvin Bean, an itinerant, albeit talented, portrait painter.

Calvin, like many of his fellow artists, earned money during the Great Depression of the 1930s by working for the WPA (Works Progress Administration), one of the numerous "alphabet agencies" that were part of President Franklin Roosevelt's "New Deal." Although painting murals and designing posters for the federal government wasn't Calvin's dream job, the WPA did provide the young man with a modest salary, something that allowed him to continue his pursuit of art for art's sake.

It was while he was painting a mural for the WPA in the

lobby of the First National Bank of Seville that he met the fair Edith. Cynics later claimed that once Calvin saw Edith's bank balance, it was love at first sight.

After courting for almost two years, Calvin finally popped the question only to drop dead the night before the wedding. Faster than a prairie fire on a windy day, the word spread through town that the thought of living in the Semple house scared the life out of poor Calvin. Even then the place was deemed to be haunted by the ghosts of Edith's tyrannical, penny-pinching parents. Now, some seventy long years later, Edith Semple had breathed her last.

In Hilly's opinion, the death was the result of old age, poverty, poor personal hygiene, and bad housekeeping. She ended the article with an assurance to her readers that Lieutenant Matt Cusak's investigation into the matter, along with the medical examiner's report, would confirm Hilly's assessment as to the actual cause of death. That alone made me suspicious.

"Yeah, and the *Titanic* was unsinkable," I remarked to the disinterested little Kees, who had settled down under the kitchen table for her postbreakfast nap. Seeing that I had nothing to offer other than caustic commentary, the pudgy pooch closed her black, shoe button–like eyes and drifted off to sleep.

Stubbing out my cigarette and dumping what was left of the coffee down the drain, I sprinted up the oak staircase to the second-floor master bathroom for a quick shower. I had a nine a.m. appointment with a prospective client, none other than Biddy McFarland herself, who was looking to convert some unused space into a handicap-friendly bedroom, bath, and sitting room. The new suite would be used by Biddy's elderly mother, who had recently given up living on her own.

Once out of the shower, I quickly dried myself off and made a series of fast passes with the dryer to my shoulder-length, gray-streaked auburn hair. A dash of blush, a hint of eye shadow, and some moisturizing lip gloss was about the extent of cosmetic enhancement that my baby boomer

face with its naturally ruddy, Irish complexion could or
would tolerate in the harsh light of day. Any additional
makeup and I would've ended up looking like Bozo the
Clown.

Since I'd already decided on my outfit the night before
(a taupe-and-cream-colored wrap dress, gold earrings, and
beige leather pumps), I managed to stay right on schedule.
I didn't want to be late knowing that like her gossip, Biddy
McFarland expected her visitors to be fresh and on time.

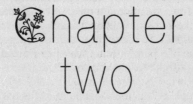

Chapter two

Because the McFarlands' manse, like all the houses in the area, was constructed before Henry Ford and his assembly line turned us into a nation of automobile owners, finding a parking spot within walking distance of the place was a hope that was fading fast. I was about to give up when to my delight, a large SUV pulled away from the curb, allowing me to park my minivan directly in front of the beautifully restored Victorian just minutes before the clock in the town square marked the hour with nine loud clangs. The din almost drowned out Biddy's gracious invitation to follow her into the old manse's formal front parlor where Vilma Beatty, Biddy's mother, was waiting for us.

"Would you care for a cup of tea or perhaps coffee?" inquired the small, birdlike woman ensconced in one of those electric scooters that, if the televised advertisements are to be believed, will restore lost mobility and allow the user to whiz around with the abandonment of a crazed drag racer.

"Thank you," I replied, "I'll have coffee if it's not too much trouble." I really didn't want or need the coffee but

I sensed that a refusal would have been taken as a social slight by Biddy's eighty-something widowed mother.

"It's no trouble at all. Bridget has it all set up," chirped Mrs. Beatty, referring to her daughter by her given name.

"Mother's right. It won't take but a minute," said Biddy, popping up from the midnight blue, velvet-covered Windsor chair that, like its twin, flanked the common brick fireplace. With her full-skirted housedress and ruffled tea apron, she reminded me of a plump June Cleaver or Harriet Nelson. "I only need to fill the teapot and coffee carafe."

With its ornately carved wood mantel and brass and iron, the fireplace was the focal point of the parlor, a room that had been updated without sacrificing the original charm of a bygone era. Gone were the dreary colors, heavy fabrics, overly ornate furniture, and inadequate lighting. There wasn't a piece of flowery bric-a-brac or an antimacassar, those little, doily-like furniture protectors, in sight. The room was done in shades of blue that ranged from pale to deep with splashes of wine red and creamy ivory accents. All the woodwork, including the crown molding, fireplace mantel, flooring, and the double pocket doors had been restored to its original golden oak glory. The room looked as warm and inviting as it did when Designer Jeans brought it back to life some two years ago.

Once Biddy had disappeared down the long corridor that led to a butler's pantry, Mrs. Beatty maneuvered the scooter across the room, bringing it to rest directly in front of the fireplace.

"You know, when I invited Bridget and my son-in-law, Gordy, to live in the house after my husband passed away, I never expected to set foot in this place again. But now I'm back and I'm afraid poor Bridget and Gordy are stuck with me just like I was stuck taking care of my father-in-law, Major Beatty," said the tiny Vilma, pointing an arthritic finger at the portrait of a bewhiskered, scowling military man that dominated the wall above the mantel. The harshness of the word "stuck" was softened by the smile on her face and the twinkle in her bright blue eyes.

"Did you know that he was the original owner of the house?" the old lady asked. Without waiting for my answer, she continued. "I think he'd be mighty pleased with how the place looks and mighty displeased with the Semple house. Why in the world Edith let that place get so bad makes about as much sense as why she wouldn't spend any of the money her parents left her. She did have some rather strange ideas."

"Are you telling me that Edith rejected her inheritance? Why on earth would she do such a thing?" I was astonished and instinctively reached in my purse for a cigarette but stopped when I remembered the THANK YOU FOR NOT SMOKING sign above the front door. For a fleeting moment, I reconsidered trying the patch.

"Because, my dear, Edith was convinced that her parents' money was the root of all evil and the love of it drove her parents to suicide. She also believed that it was the lack of money on her fiancé's part that caused his ill health and subsequent death even though the doctors told her that all the money in the world couldn't buy him a new heart. In her mind, the money was a curse, not a blessing, especially her parents' money." Vilma Beatty shook her head as if to rid it of an unwanted memory.

"If she didn't touch the money her folks left her and she didn't work, how did she manage? Maybe her fiancé had life insurance and named her as the beneficiary," I said answering my own dumb question with an even dumber answer.

Vilma Beatty smiled. "Oh, my dear girl," she said, "it was the height of the Great Depression. People were lucky if they had enough money to buy a loaf of bread much less insurance. No, Edith survived by selling off the contents of the house but only when it was absolutely necessary. Some of the items might have been valuable or increased in value over the years but of lot of it was old junk. Although, I know for a fact that . . ."

Whatever it was that Vilma Beatty was going to tell me would remain unsaid as Biddy returned from the kitchen pushing a tea cart loaded with an assortment of refreshments that would've pleased even the most finicky of guests. Biddy might be a gossip but she's also one heck of a hostess. I put her right up there with Martha Stewart. Even the napkins were the real thing—snowy white and 100 percent linen.

The stick-thin Vilma managed to devour an entire plate of petit fours while her full-figured daughter nibbled a tiny slice of unfrosted angel food cake. Biddy took her coffee black whereas Vilma put so much cream and sugar in her cup that I was surprised there was room for the tea. Once the crystal cake stand was as empty as the silver sugar bowl and creamer, it was time to get down to business. I could only hope that the differences I'd observed between mother and daughter didn't extend to their taste in decor and that I would be able to cobble together a design plan that would please them both.

To my delight and surprise, mother and daughter were in sync, giving me plenty of input, and were open to my suggestions. For the most part, what could be done in the existing second-floor bedroom and sitting room was discussed in general terms while the plan for the new bathroom was discussed in detail.

Access to the second floor could be made via the magnificent entrance hall staircase or via the recently installed elevator located off the kitchen where a servants' staircase once stood.

The elevator, bragged Biddy, was her husband Gordon's idea. "He's such a lamb about Mother's limited mobility and wants her to be as independent as possible."

No doubt this was true. But I also suspected the thought of lugging Vilma and her scooter up and down either of the steep stairways influenced the decision by the corpulent owner of McFarland's Bakery and Ice Cream Emporium to replace the back staircase with Elisha Otis's invention.

I assured Biddy that like the elevator, the new bathroom would add to Vilma's independence. I then proposed that the room have an oversized, walk-in shower with built-in seating, sturdy grip bars, and controlled hot and cold water. I made the suggestion that all the flooring in the room be of the nonslip variety. Since it was an inside room with no windows and thus no natural light, I pushed for installing a skylight and recessed can lighting with a wall-mounted dimmer switch. The dimmer switch would allow the user to adjust the intensity of light as needed. The commode, like all the cabinetry, countertops, switches, faucets, and towel and grip bars would be placed at an accessible height and be user friendly.

"Well," I said, gathering up my notes, "I think we covered all the bases. Next time we get together I should have a completed design plan along with some swatches, color charts, and samples. Fortunately, Designer Jeans's schedule is fairly flexible at the present so anytime after this coming Monday will work for JR and me. That is, if it work for you ladies."

If truth be known, Designer Jeans's schedule was as bare as a *Playboy* centerfold, but I saw no reason to share this information with Biddy and her mother.

"Really? My goodness, I thought for sure you'd be tied up for at least the next two weeks what with that terrible other business," replied Biddy with a small, knowing smile and looking as innocent as a cherub in a Renaissance painting.

"I'm sorry, but am I missing something here?" I asked in all honesty, something of a first for me. "What other business?"

I should have quit while I was ahead. Instead, I all but handed the key to Pandora's box to Biddy and her mother.

"Because, my dear"—it was Vilma Beatty's turn to smile knowingly—"Bridget says when it comes to mysteries, you can't leave them alone. She told me all about the nasty business out on Old Railway Road that you sorted out and how before that, you were instrumental in solving the murder at the country club. With your knack for sleuthing, it makes sense that Police Chief Rollie Stevens will be asking for your help. At least that's what my Bridget told me."

You and probably half the town, I said silently. The last thing I needed was to have my name linked to the Semple investigation. With Matt's mantra about being a decorator and not a detective running through my head, I made it clear to both the mother and daughter that the only thing I was interested in solving was their design problem. Or at least I hoped that I did.

"Mrs. Beatty, Biddy, let me assure you both that I will be concentrating all my energy on the task at hand, which is to turn unused space into a gracious, usable, and handicap-accessible suite. Now, if you will excuse me, I really must be going. I have a lot of things to do and believe me, they are all design related."

The last sentence was delivered with Bette Davis–like fortitude (the kind she displayed in *Now, Voyager*) in an effort to squelch even the slightest hint to the contrary. On that dramatic note, I took my leave.

Too bad Charlie and Matt weren't on hand to hear my declaration. I felt sure that had they been there, I would have received a standing ovation. Only later would I realize that not receiving applause from my husband or my son-in-law would be the least of my problems.

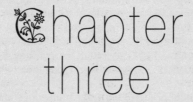Chapter three

Upon leaving the McFarland residence, I resisted the urge to stop and touch base with Officer Patti Crump, who was guarding the Semple premises. Instead, I got into the mini-van and was in the process of pulling away from the curb when I caught sight of the unmarked police car in my rearview mirror. The vehicle came to a halt in front of the Semple house. I watched as my police lieutenant son-in-law quickly alighted from the car along with the driver—Matt's trusted sidekick, the bald and stoic Sergeant Sid Rosen. I did wonder what was going on but true to my word, I put my nose in the air, reminded myself that I wasn't Seville's answer to Christie's Hercule Poirot, and headed for JR and Matt's 1920s renovated bungalow on Tall Timber Road.

Pulling into the long driveway, I was greeted by JR and the latest addition to the family, baby Charles Matthew Cusak, who was born the year before on Christmas Day. In a moment of parental weakness, JR and Matt gave in to their ten-year-old twins' (Kerry, a girl, and Kelly, a boy) request that they be allowed to give their new baby brother a suitable nickname. Among the names the twins seriously considered were Santa, Rudolph, Frosty, Alf, Tiny Tim, and the easy to spell Xmas. When the parents regained their senses and control, they settled the matter by bestowing the moniker of Kris on the baby.

Safely snuggled in JR's arms, Kris gave me a toothless smile and gurgled contentedly. With his black, curly hair and his big, gold-flecked, blue green eyes, the little guy is a combination of the tall, dark, and handsome Matt and the willowy, blond, and bonny JR. Kris also has a sweet personality, which is a nice change from the twins' natural contrariness.

Over a pitcher of iced tea and a platter of tuna fish salad sandwiches, I filled JR in on the McFarland project. She was both excited and apprehensive since the project would be long and involved due to a dependency on subcontractors and outside suppliers. She was somewhat cheered by the news that I expected the project to be a satisfying, positive experience for the client and a profitable one for Designer Jeans.

"Gee," said JR, "do you think Aunt Mary meant it when she volunteered to watch the baby should I find myself in need of a sitter? The twins won't be a problem since they'll be starting school the week after summer camp wraps up. Maybe I should give her a call in case she changed her mind about the offer."

"You can call her if you want to, but I'm sure that she wouldn't have said it if she didn't mean it. If Matt has no problem with Kris spending time in a playpen set up in Mary's office down at the furniture store, then you have nothing to worry about, except maybe you'll end up with a baby influenced not by Dr. Spock but Mr. Spock," I joked, taking the opportunity to remind JR of England's Fine Furniture salesman Herbie Waddlemeyer's obsession with UFOs and close encounters of the third kind. The guy is a real space cadet.

Apparently my daughter is more open-minded than her mother. Ignoring my remark, she asked if Biddy McFarland had anything to say about Edith Semple's passing.

She was surprised and pleased when I told her Biddy had little to say on the subject. I figured Biddy's comment about the possibility of my investigating the case wasn't worth mentioning.

"Thank God for small favors," JR said as she settled baby Kris in his high chair in preparation for feeding him his lunch. "Matt says it really upsets him when some ill-informed airhead tries to turn a natural death into a homicide."

Opening the jar of baby food, JR began spooning its contents into Kris's waiting, open mouth. The jar's label depicted a pink-and-blue horn of plenty overflowing with a magnificent variety of luscious-looking vegetables. This caused me to question truth in advertising since the gook Kris was gobbling down had the consistency of sludge and smelled almost as bad.

Seeking to put some distance between me, the jar of baby food, and the airhead remark, I moved from my place at the table and leaned against the kitchen counter.

"So was Hilly right about the cause of death?" I asked, helping myself to a second glass of iced tea and a rather nondescript-looking cookie.

"Not really. She definitely was wrong about the poor personal hygiene and bad housekeeping. Matt said that although the house was terribly run-down, it was surprisingly neat and clean, as was Edith. Dr. Sue Lin Loo phoned Matt this morning with the confirmation that Edith died from a massive, cerebral hemorrhage. According to Loo, and since she's the medical examiner she ought to know, even if help had been available, the outcome probably would've been the same since that type of stroke is almost always fatal."

That Hilly Murrow was wrong about Edith's personal habits and housekeeping skills made me feel somewhat better but not much. I knew the *Sentinel* wouldn't bother printing a retraction, thus leaving the citizens of Seville with the mistaken belief that Edith was a poverty-stricken, slovenly old woman who died wallowing in squalor. I was

about to sample the cookie when JR reached over and took
it out of my hand.

"Thanks, Mom," she said, presenting the cookie to the
drooling Kris. "Look what Mama's got for her big boy—
your favorite teething biscuit."

With his eyes opened almost as wide as his wet mouth,
Kris grabbed onto the rock-hard pastry. He then proceeded
to clamp down on the thing with all the vigor, strength,
and tenacity of a shark in a feeding frenzy. In no time at
all, Kris managed to spread the drippings from the biscuit
in his hair, on his face, and down the front of his once
spotless bib where it mixed with the vegetable sludge, thus
creating a gastronomical mess of epic proportions.

When JR and Kris headed for the bathroom for a scrub
down and complete change of clothes for both mother and
child, I grabbed the roll of paper towels and a full bottle of
all-purpose kitchen cleaner. Working to return the high
chair and floor to their prebaby lunch condition, I silently
wondered if my best friend and sister-in-law, Mary Hastings England, realized what she was letting herself in for
with her generous offer to babysit Kris and at England's
Fine Furniture no less. I also wondered if the furniture in
Mary's office was as washable as baby Kris.

A few minutes later, JR returned to the kitchen minus
the baby, who had been put in his crib for an afternoon
nap. "Thanks for cleaning up the high chair and floor. I
sure hope Aunt Mary knows what a job she's taking on
with her offer to watch the baby while I'm tied up with the
project."

"Listen, after raising her own tribe of boys, Mary can
handle Kris. But there is one thing that does worry me
some," I teased, putting a fresh roll of paper towels in the
holder and tossing the now empty bottle of all-purpose
cleaner in the trash.

"Oh my gosh, like what?" cried JR, sounding every bit
as concerned as she looked.

"I worry that she'll run out of paper towels and spray
cleaner before Kris runs out of baby food and teething

biscuits." I laughed but JR didn't. Sometimes she's so much like her father. Obviously, this was one of those times.

I kissed JR good-bye and headed for Kettle Cottage, my own modest English-style cottage. It was designed and built in the late 1940s by Archibald Kettle, a gifted architect and dedicated Anglophile. When my husband and I purchased it some thirty-plus years ago, the townspeople had already christened it Kettle Cottage and the name stuck. With luck, I'd be home in time to watch *Sunset Boulevard*, starring Gloria Swanson and William Holden. The film was being shown on the classic movie channel. Unlike Swanson's Norma Desmond, I wasn't ready for my close-up but I was ready for a glass of wine, a cigarette, and William Holden.

That evening Charlie and I arrived at the Sleepy Hollow Country Club for our dinner date with Mary and Denny England. The clubhouse, located on a high bluff at the edge of town, was built in the 1920s. Architecturally, with its white stucco exterior, arched porticos, and orange tile roof, the club is a prime example of early twentieth-century California kitsch.

We were greeted at the double glass-panel entrance doors of the main dining room by the delightfully ditzy, attractive hostess, Tammie Flowers. "Evenin' Mr. H., Mrs. H.," said the curvaceous redhead, speaking in her own unique form of verbal shorthand. "Lookin' good, Mrs. H., ditto, Mr. H. The Es are waitin' for you. Follow me and I'll take you to their table."

Crossing the black-and-white checkerboard tile floor, I felt a twinge of pride that the Art Deco decor looked as sleek and cosmopolitan as it did when Designer Jeans restored the room to its former glory three years ago.

As we neared the table, the gentlemanly Denny stood up, waiting for me to be seated. With his crinkly blue eyes, fringe of steely gray hair, and windburned face, the tall and lanky Scotsman looks more like a man of the sea than the owner of a landlocked furniture store in the popcorn capital of America.

Not to be outdone by his brother-in-law's display of good manners, Charlie attempted to pull out a chair for me only to be stopped by Tammie. "Sorry, Mr. H., but that's my job. You and Mr. E. can set yourselves down while I see to Mrs. H."

Once Tammie was satisfied that everyone had been properly seated, she wiggled back to the podium by the frosted double doors where she enthusiastically greeted the latest arrivals, a dour-looking man and woman.

"Wanna bet that by the time she gets them settled in their chairs, they'll be all smiles," declared Mary as she watched the elderly couple follow the voluptuous former waitress to a cozy table set for two on the far side of the room.

The short and pleasingly plump Mary looked terrific in a new navy-and-white pantsuit. The suit was complemented by a pair of red patent leather, sling-back shoes and large, silver hoop earrings. Mary's mass of snowy white curls had been clipped short for the summer. The easy-to-care-for style called attention to her peaches-and-cream complexion, dimpled smile, and big, blueberry-colored eyes.

Thanks to my addiction to classic movies, I'd had less than five minutes to get ready for dinner. The wrap dress I'd slipped into that morning looked less than fresh but I was counting on the dining room's soft lighting to diminish the spots and wrinkles. I breathed a sigh of relief when no one commented on my less-than-stellar appearance.

Mary and I engaged in small talk that lasted through our salads and entrees, but by the time dessert was served, the conversation had drifted into more serious waters initiated by my bringing up the subject of the McFarland project.

After reassuring me that she would be delighted to watch the baby for JR, Mary wanted to know what Biddy had to say regarding Edith Semple's death. Denny and Charlie had been conducting their own conversation, which naturally centered on golf, but stopped in mid-sentence to hear my answer.

"Nothing much other than a few negative comments directed at the condition of the Semple property," I informed my disbelieving audience of three.

"That in itself is suspicious, kind of like Edith's death, wouldn't you agree, Gin?" commented Mary between spoonfuls of chunky peppermint ice cream and calling me by my childhood nickname that I'd like to forget and Mary can't or won't.

"Not at all. Only an ill-informed airhead would think that Edith Semple's death was a homicide," I replied, taking my son-in-law's words and making them my own.

Mary looked disappointed, Denny looked satisfied, and Charlie looked suspicious. What I just said didn't jive with what I'd said to Charlie that morning. He was aware of this and was about to bring it to my attention when I was saved by Ben Kind.

In addition to being the president and owner of the B. Kind Sure Mortgage Company, Ben was also head of the Sleepy Hollow Country Club men's golf league. Tall and portly, the perpetually cheerful, fifty-something Ben had stopped by our table to introduce the four of us to his dinner guest, Stuart Goodenough. Mr. Goodenough, Ben quickly informed us, was a successful real estate broker from Castle Hills, one of Indianapolis's most exclusive suburbs.

Although his hair was more gray than brown and his hazel eyes didn't exactly sparkle, the well-dressed, stocky, middle-aged Stuart—as he invited us to call him—had a magnetic personality that more than made up for what he lacked in the looks department. The twice-divorced broker kept the conversation bright, light, and interesting before Ben managed to steer it in the direction of an upcoming golf outing.

Ten mind-numbing minutes later, the long-winded Ben finally bid us farewell and with his guest in tow, headed for the bar located in the west wing of the club house. By then,

Mary and I'd had our fill of ice cream, coffee, and golf talk. Like our husbands, we were ready to call it a night, leaving the subject of Edith Semple's passing as dead as the woman herself.

Chapter four

Unlike the McFarland project, the Semple investigation was over almost before it began. With no signs of forced entry, robbery, or foul play and with Dr. Sue Lin Loo's finding of death due to natural causes, Edith Semple's earthly body was quietly buried in the Seville cemetery.

The entire time Designer Jeans was working on the McFarland project, which was most of the summer, I made it my business to keep Biddy informed as to how things were or were not progressing with Vilma's new suite. The biggest problem was dovetailing Designer Jeans's schedule with delivery dates and the availability of materials and workers.

Biddy, in turn, made it her business to keep me informed as to how things were or were not progressing with the settlement of the Semple estate. This she did in spite of my disinterest in the subject, something I had made her aware of from the start.

According to Biddy, the Chicago-born Danny Semple (aka Danny Danger) a rising heavy-metal rock musician and a distant relative of the Semples, inherited everything including the dilapidated house and its contents.

"I'm not one to spread rumors," said Biddy piously, clasping her hands to her ample bosom, "but from what I hear, this Danny person is not exactly a model for today's youngsters. When he's not performing at some outdoor concert, he's in drug rehab. I suspect he won't be making Seville his home base so the place will probably be put on the market, although I can't imagine anyone in their right mind buying the place. Heaven knows how much longer I'll have to put up with living next door to that horrible, old eyesore of a house."

Anxious to get back to the supervising of the installation of the special-order shower surround in the new bathroom, and with JR waiting for the paint I'd picked up at the local home center store, I didn't have time for Biddy's gossip.

"Maybe you'll luck out and somebody will buy the place and flip it," I said, referring to the practice of a quick and economical renovation of a property with the object of making a hefty profit on a fast turnaround sale while the market is hot.

"Flip it? I've never heard of such a thing," squawked Biddy as I stepped inside the little elevator off the McFarland's kitchen and pushed the up button. The door slid closed, leaving Biddy on her own to ponder the fate of the Semple manse.

The following day, JR and I were on our way to England's Fine Furniture to have lunch with Mary and Kris. As expected, traffic was heavy and parking difficult. Like most Hoosiers, the people of Seville would sooner skip lunch at the White House than miss sitting down for their noonday meal with family and/or friends.

After dropping JR off at the furniture store, I continued my search for a parking spot. As my minivan circled the block, I caught a red light near the town square. Waiting for the light to turn green, I watched as Biddy McFarland and Amanda Little (Seville's most successful real estate agent) shared an outside table at the Koffee Kabin. There wasn't any doubt in my mind that by the time the two finished lunch, Biddy would have the lowdown on flipping as well as what the future might hold for a certain recently vacated, supposedly haunted, decrepit old Victorian mansion.

I arrived at Mary's office in time to grab a slice of cold pizza, which I washed down with a can of warm soda. So much for lunch. But the sight of Kris enjoying his mother's company while JR and Mary enjoyed most of the once piping hot pizza from Milano's (our town's best and only Italian restaurant) made the break in the workday worthwhile.

On our way out of the store, Herbie Waddlemeyer gave me the good news that the furniture and Tiffany-style lamps Designer Jeans had ordered for Vilma's sitting room were in and available for delivery. Although there was still work to be done on the project, things were finally starting to gel and I could see light at the end of the tunnel. Perhaps, I thought, Designer Jeans would be able to finish the McFarland project sooner rather than later.

From that point on, the project proceeded without a hitch, including the plumbing and electrical work along with the installation of the skylight and new flooring. All the workers showed up as promised as did the special-order tile, cabinetry, and fixtures for the bathroom. Even the trompe l'oeil café scene I'd planned for the walls of the sitting room was finished on time and trouble free thanks to JR's artistic ability and steady hand.

A week shy of the Labor Day holiday, Vilma Beatty was enjoying the luxury and independence of her own private suite, JR was back to being a full-time mommy, and I was left (figuratively speaking) sitting in Kettle Cottage counting flowers on the wall. Of course that all changed when the telephone rang and I found Designer Jeans being offered a deal that I couldn't refuse.

"And that's all I have to do. That's it? Consulting and staging and a bit of painting? Sure, I'm interested," I said, unable to keep the surprise or excitement out of my voice.

My caller was Amanda Little and we agreed to meet for

lunch the following day in the country club's bar and grill where the offer would be discussed in detail. When she hung up, I wasted no time throwing the two frozen turkey and dressing entrees back in the freezer. I then rushed into the den and announced to Charlie that we would be going out for dinner.

"What's the occasion? Don't tell me there's some new holiday I missed. You know I still have my doubts about that Sweetest Day business. That little surprise cost me a dozen long-stemmed roses and a box of Godiva chocolates," said Charlie as he checked his computer for the latest e-mail.

"For your information, chum, Sweetest Day is a legitimate holiday. If you don't believe me, look at my Hallmark calendar. Now, getting back to the subject of dinner, I thought you would like to help celebrate the lucrative offer Amanda Little just presented to me. She wants me, or I should say Designer Jeans, to consult on decor and stage a house she's handling for a quick sale or as they call it in real estate circles, a flip."

"You want to run that by me again. What do you mean stage a house? It sounds like she wants you to put on a play or something. I don't want to hurt your feelings, but to be honest about it sweetheart, while you're one heck of an old movie buff, you're not much of an actress."

"Really? Personally, I've always thought my takeoff on Bette Davis was pretty good, and my mother once told me that I reminded her of Maureen O'Hara," I shot back, not bothering to explain to Charlie that at the time, she was referring to my Irish temper.

"Okay, you win. Now would you care to explain to me exactly what staging means. Call me cheap but I like to know what I'm celebrating before I order the champagne."

"Think of the word stage as a verb and not a noun," I said, sounding more like a teacher than an interior designer. "As such, it is a presentation of a few well-placed pieces and accessories that hint what can be done with the space and its use. Do you know what I'm saying?" I paused and lit a cigarette, giving Charlie a chance to digest my explanation.

"Yeah, I think I do." He laughed. "In other words, staging is what allows a husband to imagine a pool table occupying the same area that his wife envisions a baby grand piano."

"You got that right. Any more questions?" I asked, not expecting the barrage that followed regarding the who, what, where, how, when, and why of Amanda's offer. "Jeez, I don't know the details, at least not yet. That's why I'm meeting her for lunch tomorrow at the club. The important thing is, Amanda Little needs my interior design skills and I need the work. Either I take her up on the offer or I take up golf with you and Denny."

"Give me five minutes to get ready, sweetheart," replied Charlie as he made a mad dash for the upstairs bedroom and a quick change of clothes, "and we'll celebrate Designer Jeans's latest project."

"See, Pesty," I said to the eavesdropping Kees, "you don't have to fight fire with fire or logic with logic. Sometimes plain old fear does the trick. Now if you're a good girl and don't splash water from your dish all over the floor while I'm gone, I'll bring you a little something from Milano's."

Upon hearing this, the little ball of fuzz flicked her furry, teddy bear–like ears and trotted into the kitchen. Instead of curling up under the table, Pesty sat herself down next to her food dish. I knew that she would stay there until I returned with the promised treat—Papa Milano's creamy, spumoni ice cream.

Chapter five

The following day, I arrived at the Sleepy Hollow Country Club on time for my lunch date with Seville's chamber of commerce's golden girl and favorite real estate agent, Amanda Little. Expecting to meet her in the bar and grill, I started down the west wing where I encountered Tammie, the club's hostess.

"Hi there, Mrs. H. Are you here for Ms. L.'s luncheon?" the ditzy redhead asked, using what I've come to think of as Tammie-speak. "'Cuz if you are, you're going in the wrong direction. It's being held in the main dining room and if I counted right, you're the last one here."

Thinking that Tammie was confused, I began to explain to her that I was having lunch with Amanda Little, who was probably waiting for me in the bar and grill.

"Oh shoot, Mrs. H. When Mac," said Tammie, referring to Tom MacNulty, the club's manager, "found out that this was a business luncheon, he had me set it up in the dining room so that you people would have some privacy. I'm on my way to turn in the drink order at the bar. I'll add a glass of Webber's Bay Chardonnay to it for you. By the time you set yourself down, I'll be back with the drinks and hors d'oeuvres."

Having said that, Tammie wiggled her way to the bar, leaving me on my own to figure out what the heck was going on. Hors d'oeuvres? Nobody in Seville has hors d'oeuvres unless it's a special occasion like a retirement party, wedding, or funeral. Good lord, I wondered, what had I gotten myself into this time?

Making my way to the dining room located in the rotunda, I began having second thoughts about Amanda's seemingly terrific offer. While my Irish intuition told me to skip the whole thing, my natural curiosity won out.

Entering the dining room, I found myself being greeted by Amanda, who, as usual, was decked out in white and gold. The natural blond with her green eyes and flawless, ivory skin looked fantastic. She proceeded to inform me that we would be having lunch with new friends and some longtime business associates.

Seating at the large, round, white linen–covered table was as follows: me, Amanda Little, Stuart Goodenough, Ben Kind, Duke Demarco (a local general contractor), and a mismatched married couple that I'd never met before. In all, there were seven people present for what Stuart proclaimed as a luncheon meeting of the Fast Flippers, whose members could expect a generous return on their investment in a buy-low, fast-fix-up, and quick-sell-high housing market—a practice known as flipping.

I was about to protest that I was neither a member of that group nor did I wish to join it when the smiling Stuart asked everyone to welcome their distinguished guest, Jean Hastings of Designer Jeans. It's hard to protest anything when one is being applauded.

Once the smattering of applause died down, Amanda introduced me to the couple, a Mr. Harry Eastwood and his wife, Bambi. And yes, Bambi was Mrs. Eastwood's given name. I guessed that the slightly built, balding Harry was on the far side of sixty unlike his tall, robust wife who looked to be barely out of her teens and barely into her clothes.

Like myself, Duke Demarco was not a member of the Fast Flippers. He and I were there because, as Stuart explained to everyone, we were vital and necessary components of the flip project.

I'd been called a lot of things over the years but never a necessary, vital component. I must admit, I was flattered. In spite of some initial hesitancy on my part regarding the group and its purpose, I found myself warming up to both.

From what I gathered, in addition to being a successful real estate broker, Stuart had a successful track record in the high-stakes game of house flipping. Because of his experience, his fellow investors had agreed that Stuart would handle such details as finding the property and arranging for a mortgage to purchase the property along with any construction loans needed for the remodel. He also would be overseeing the project from start to finish.

Ben Kind beamed benevolently as Stuart informed everyone that the B. Kind Sure Mortgage Company was ready and eager to work with Stuart and the group in obtaining an interest-only mortgage for the flip property. He was also setting up an account that Stuart, as the overseer of the project, could draw from to cover renovation expenses.

Amanda Little would handle the resale of the hot property once it was redone and placed back on the market. For this, she could expect to receive a lucrative commission when the house was sold.

Duke Demarco would be the general contractor for the remodel part of the flip. As such, the beefy, easygoing, middle-aged Duke would deal with suppliers, schedules, subcontractors, workers, and any on-the-job problems.

Last but not least, Designer Jeans would be responsible for design and decorating ideas, help in the selection of various items such as flooring, cabinetry, a bit of specialty painting, and the staging of the property for the resale.

A smiling Stuart Goodenough looked around the table and asked if there were any questions. I was about to inquire exactly what hot property was going to be flipped but was usurped by Bambi, whose squeal was as unsettling as a civil defense siren during a Midwest thunderstorm.

"Stuart, honey, Harry just told me that Danny Danger sold us that old dump we're going to flip. Man, he's sooo hot," shrieked Bambi. "Do you think he'll come and see it when it's all done?"

"I doubt that very much, my dear," Stuart replied with a snort. "Apparently Danny is a very superstitious fellow and believer in things that go bump in the night. Upon learning that he'd inherited a supposedly haunted house, he instructed his attorneys to get rid of it, including its contents, ASAP, so they put the 'old dump' on the market and priced it for a quick sale. The low price, coupled with a hot market for renovated Victorians, makes it the perfect candidate for flipping. With the fortune he inherited as the only surviving relative of the Semples, and with the way his career has taken off, that young man won't be coming to Seville anytime soon, if ever."

"Bummer," declared the crestfallen Bambi, "but it's true that he really believes in all that ghost stuff. He even sprinkles the stage with salt before every performance just to keep ghosts and evil spirits away. I saw him do that with my own eyes in Vegas."

With her head of frizzy, bleached hair, an overabundance of eye makeup, and skimpy attire, Bambi Eastwood looked like a pouting Barbie doll. The former exotic dancer also looked closer to thirty than twenty as I'd originally thought.

"Now, now, Bambi," scolded Harry Eastwood, sounding more like a father than a husband, "that's all part of his act like his jumping out of a casket, hanging himself with an electrical cord, falling into a vat of acid, leaping into a burning inferno, and smashing his guitar with karate chops."

"How awful. I'm glad to say I've never seen his act and

have no intention of doing so," declared the prudish Ben Kind. "These so-called musicians like this fellow are an absolute disgrace."

Interrupting Ben Kind's dissertation on the decline of morality in modern society, Amanda Little proposed a toast to Stuart Goodenough for giving others the opportunity to share in the flipping phenomenon.

From the way that the darling of Seville's town council looked at the guy, it was clear to me that Amanda's interest in him went beyond the speedy makeover and resale of the Semple house. For the forty-something, never-been-married Amanda Little's sake, I hoped the feeling was mutual. I also hoped that the hinky feeling I was beginning to have about Stuart Goodenough was as wrong as Ben Kind's opinion of today's youth.

Before Stuart arrived on the scene, the town gossips had spread the word that Arthur Kraft, owner of Kraft Flowers and a town councilman, was courting the fair Amanda. While it was true that the bashful bachelor asked Amanda to help out at the council's annual fish fry, I would hardly classify spending an afternoon together dispensing beer-battered catfish to hungry townsfolk as a date.

At the conclusion of the meeting and the lunch that followed, I invited the beautiful real estate agent to stop in the bar for a drink. I'd hoped to talk to her about my role in the flipping project. I also thought Amanda might be able to give me some background info on the Eastwoods and Stuart Goodenough. But when she asked for a rain check and dashed off to a business appointment, I skipped the bar altogether where, interestingly enough, Arthur Kraft was seated. Instead, I headed for my van in the club's parking lot. In doing so, I caught up with the Eastwoods.

Talking as we walked along, I was able to learn from the affable Harry, a retired manufacturer of plastics, that he and Bambi had recently settled in Seville after selling their luxurious Las Vegas condo. At present, they were renting a mid-twentieth-century ranch house on the far edge of town. The reason for the relocation was to be closer to the Indianapolis hospice where Harry's mother was spending her final days. That the move also brought them in close proximity to where his former wife and grown daughter resided was, in Harry's words, a bonus. I didn't need to be told how Bambi felt about the matter. The sullen look on her face spoke volumes.

Since Harry was in such a talkative mood, I thought it was an opportune time to ask how and when he'd become acquainted with Stuart Goodenough.

"Actually, I met him shortly after moving to Indiana. It was at an Indianapolis medical center where we were both waiting to see the same doctor," said Harry. Bambi was with me at the time and struck up a conversation with Mr. Goodenough. When she commented on the lack of night-life in Seville, Stuart offered to show us what Indy had to offer. Thanks to him, Bambi has adjusted to our relocation to Indiana better than I'd hoped."

I could've made a couple of comments of my own but good sense and manners prevailed.

"Harry!" screeched Bambi, giving her husband a whack with her oversized designer purse, "I want to go home *now*!"

Like a dog on a short leash, Harry responded to her command and hurriedly escorted Bambi to their car, which was parked nearby. As I climbed into my van, the East-woods' BMW sped past, showering me and my van with a spray of finely crushed gravel. I knew without looking that Bambi was in the driver's seat.

Chapter six

Once the Semple house renovation was under way it proceeded at breathtaking speed. Periodically, JR and I were
summoned to the job site or a supply center where we
would meet with Duke Demarco and Stuart Goodenough
for the purpose of lending our expertise in the design and
decor needed to complete the flip on time and on budget.

Like everyone who had the opportunity to visit the Semple place during the high-speed remodel, I was impressed
with how great the old place was starting to look. The outside had been given a new roof, siding, front porch, stairs,
brick walkway, and some much needed landscaping.

While the old house retained its Victorian flavor on the
outside, the inside was a totally different story. Gone was
the maze of tiny rooms that had been connected by a series
of dark hallways. The second floor originally consisted of
two small bedrooms and a partial attic. At Designer Jeans's
suggestion, the area had been transformed into a master
suite, guest bedroom, and a bonus room. With the exception of the master bath, the entire second floor received
new, wall-to-wall beige carpeting.

All the walls, both upstairs and down, were stripped of peeling wallpaper, then painted in soft shades of colors taken from an earth-tone palette. We'd selected this particular palette knowing that it would appeal to the majority of prospective buyers.

Designer Jeans also suggested a radical transformation of the main floor's dingy and outdated kitchen, dark and formal dining room, and two small parlors into bright and spacious areas. To achieve this open concept, non-load-bearing walls were removed. This allowed the new kitchen and dining area, along with the new family room, to flow into the new, inviting living room. With help from Duke Demarco, we even managed to squeeze in a combination bath and laundry room in our plan for new use of old, poorly used space.

In a move to keep cost down, we chose the same simple white cabinetry with frosted glass doors and quartz composite countertops for the kitchen and new bathrooms. That the engineered stone looked great with the kitchen's new, stainless steel appliances and backsplash came as no surprise to me or JR.

Thanks to Duke Demarco and the people he hired for the cleanup and restoration, all the changes Designer Jeans had suggested were speedily and faithfully executed.

Although I knew the time was drawing near for staging the house, I didn't realize just how near until Amanda Little telephoned me late one Thursday afternoon with the news that the all-important open house was scheduled for the coming Sunday.

Since I was in my kitchen at the time, I'd taken the call on Charlie's latest eBay purchase, which was an enormous Mickey Mouse telephone. When I objected on the grounds that the phone clashed with the room's Tuscan decor, he reminded me that I'd objected to its predecessor, a Day-Glo pink monstrosity, and had insisted that anything else would be better. The new phone was Charlie's interpretation of better.

"Sunday? That doesn't give me much time to pull it all

together," I protested to the anxious Amanda even though I knew that with JR's help the staging could be done in a day.

"Sorry for the short notice," Amanda replied, "but it's Stuart, not me who's insisting on holding the open house this Sunday. First, he pushed Duke Demarco almost to the breaking point to get the place finished by today and now he's pushing me to get the place sold. I dread to think what's going to happen if Sunday's open house turns out to be a bust."

Poor Amanda Little. She sounded so disheartened, I did my best to assure her that Designer Jeans was up to the task of staging the house in one day—Friday.

I also did my best to inject some humor into the conversation. "Now that that's been settled, how would you like to take a sneak peek at the place on Saturday? That way there won't be any surprises on Sunday."

"Surprises? Like what?" challenged the puzzled real estate agent, unaware that she'd fallen into my trap.

"Like the life-size, nude sculpture of Bambi Eastwood. It's the first thing potential buyers will see when they enter the house. Not only is the piece warm and welcoming, it's also very realistic, right down to the belly button ring."

"You've got to be kidding," gasped the shocked Amanda. "I've already seen quite enough of Bambi Eastwood. It seems every time I turn around, she's there, especially when I'm with Stuart. Please, Jean, tell me you're kidding."

"Yes, I am," I admitted before adding, "the sculpture is only three feet high and it's of Harry, not Bambi, but the rest of it's all true, even the belly button ring. Would I lie?"

Once we both got our laughter under control, we said our good-byes but not before agreeing to meet at the Semple manse on Saturday evening, around six, for Amanda's pre–open house walk through. The always busy Amanda set the time, claiming she couldn't possibly make it earlier due to a few things that she had to personally take care of, including one that, if not handled properly, could come back to haunt her.

Returning the phone to its base, I could've sworn that the smile on Mickey's face had gone from sunny to sinister. The fact that a certain little Keeshond was growling at the thing wasn't helping matters.

Convinced that I was suffering from brain overload, I gave both Mickey and Pesty an affectionate pat on the head and put my overactive imagination on hold for the time being.

Chapter seven

~❦~

"Tonsillitis?" I all but shouted into the phone. After the smiling incident with the Disney icon telephone, I thought it best to give it a rest and used my cell phone to contact JR. While I expected her to be surprised at the news regarding the open house being set for Sunday, I didn't expect her to surprise me with some news of her own.

"Mother, if you don't calm down, I'm going to hang up," JR informed me in her no-nonsense voice. "Doc Parker says it seems to be a fairly uncomplicated case but until it runs its course, he wants Matt to stay in bed and I'm stuck playing nurse."

"Jeez, I'm sorry, JR, but you really took me by surprise. Like most people, when I hear tonsillitis I think kids, not grown-ups and certainly not someone Matt's age and size."

"The worst part of the whole thing is the porcelain bell Kerry and Kelly gave him. Now, whenever Matt needs something really, really important like the sports section of the newspaper, the *TV Guide*, or a Popsicle he rings that damn bell."

I was about to give my daughter some heartfelt sympathy when the ringing of said bell brought a halt to my side of the conversation.

"I better go and see what Quasimodo wants now before he wakes up the baby," grumbled JR.

Sensing that my daughter was in no mood to discuss memorable literary characters, I let her reference to Victor Hugo's mad bell ringer pass without comment.

"Hey, have you thought about asking Aunt Mary to give you a hand with the staging, Mom? I bet she would. Give her a call. Love ya. Bye."

"Yeah, either her or Biddy McFarland," I remarked facetiously to Pesty, who was keeping one eye on her food dish and the other on Mickey Mouse. "I'll bet Biddy would be willing to do just about anything to see what's been going on inside the Semple house."

With Pesty playing watchdog, I sat back, lit a cigarette, and weighed the pros and cons of involving my best friend and sister-in-law, the vulnerable Mary Hastings England, in Designer Jeans's latest project.

On the plus side was Mary's unflagging enthusiasm and eagerness to help those in need.

On the minus side was Mary's unflagging enthusiasm and eagerness to help those in need.

Mary had been instrumental in getting her husband, Denny England, to agree to my "borrowing" items needed to stage the Semple house from England's Fine Furniture's supply of floor samples and decorative accessories. She even managed to get Denny, a true Scotsman, to throw in free delivery and pickup.

"Give a yell when you're ready and Herbie will be there with the goods," Mary had informed me.

In view of all that she'd already done for Designer Jeans, I decided that I couldn't impose on her more. Instead, I would emulate the ultimate survivor, the indefatigable Little Red Hen of nursery book fame, and do it all myself.

I was still savoring my spunky decision to go it alone

when I heard the sound of Denny England's ancient sports car pulling into the driveway, followed by the sound of Charlie's voice as he bid his brother-in-law good-bye. Charlie and Denny had signed up for Sleepy Hollow's annual fall golf outing. The outing included a golf tournament, a sit-down dinner, and an evening of low-stakes card games.

"Charlie! I didn't expect you home so early," I yelped as he stomped into the kitchen. "Is something wrong?"

"You bet there's something wrong. Guess who me and Denny got stuck golfing with? I'll give you a hint. It wasn't Honest Abe, that's for damn sure." Charlie's handsome face was dark with anger.

Pesty, fearing her latest pastry raid might have something to do with Charlie's wrath, sought shelter under the kitchen table. She was almost positive that the stale doughnut hole she'd devoured hadn't been missed but she was unsure about the three oatmeal cookies. Like all Keeshonds, the little fuzz ball was not about to put herself in jeopardy. She would stay under the table until Charlie's verbal storm passed or dinner was served, whichever came first.

"For chrissake, the way he kept score for himself and Ben Kind, no wonder they ended up in the money. And they say cheaters never win. Well, take it from me, he sure did. Denny and I were so disgusted, we left as soon as the dinner was over. I wanted to say something to Ben about the guy but Denny talked me out of it."

"I assume that you're upset with Ben's golf partner whose last name isn't Lincoln," I said, crushing out my cigarette and silently reviewing my dinner options. With an irate husband on my hands, I thought it best to stay home. I could either call for a pizza or fix myself a couple of grilled cheese sandwiches. I was trying to make up my mind when Charlie referred to the golf cheat by his proper name—Stuart Goodenough.

In less than one hour, I'd learned more about Stuart Goodenough than in all the hours JR and I had spent fulfilling our part of the flip. Now, thanks to Amanda Little's phone call and Charlie's tirade, I knew the always smiling, smooth-talking guy was both a bully and a cheat. But was he also a charlatan? Would he make good on his promise to pay the balance of the money he owed Designer Jeans once the Semple manse was staged and ready for the open house? My Irish intuition kicked in and this time I wasn't about to ignore it.

"Excuse me, Charlie, but I need to call your sister, Mary, about tomorrow. I'm going to be staging the Semple house. It's not that big of a job but to be on the safe side, I think I'll ask Mary to give me a hand."

I waited until Charlie had helped himself to a short stack of oatmeal cookies and a glass of milk and had headed for the den before I reached for the phone. Throwing a napkin over Mickey's grinning face, I dialed Mary's home phone number. As usual, the call was answered by both Mary and voice mail.

"Hello . . . hello? What the heck? My stars, I can't seem to . . . oops, sorry caller. Please hold. I'll be with you in a moment," said Mary, struggling to take control of the telephone call. "Okay, go ahead, caller. You have reached your party," she chirped.

That the former Ma Bell long-distance operator had triumphed so quickly over technology, I took as a positive sign that Mary was catching up with the world around her.

"Mar, it's me, Jean," I volunteered, anxious to get on with my request. "I need a favor and was wondering if maybe you could help me out. If the answer's no, I'll understand."

"Of course I'll help you out. What is it you want me to do? Give JR a hand? She certainly has her hands full with Matt being sick and all. I told her to bring the baby down to the store. I really miss the little guy. So does Herbie. He's so adorable."

"Who? Herbie Waddlemeyer?" I couldn't resist playing straight man to the unsuspecting Mary.

"No, silly. I was referring to baby Kris although Herbie is an awfully nice person and a wonderful employee."

"Yeah, right. Listen, Mary, what I called about has nothing to do with JR's problems other than she's unable to help me stage the Semple house tomorrow. I thought if you're free, maybe you could lend me a hand."

"No problem, Gin. You're also going to need all that stuff that Denny set aside for you. I'll ride over to the house with Herbie in the delivery truck. We should be there by eight tomorrow morning. Does that work for you?"

"More than you can ever imagine," I replied. "I'll be waiting for you and the adorable Herbie with rings on my fingers and bells on my toes."

"Speaking for myself, Gin, I would much rather find you waiting with a couple of hot coffees in one hand and a box of fresh doughnuts in the other. If you're smart, you'll leave the fingers and toes bling-bling to the likes of Bambi Eastwood. Gossip has it that if it wasn't for her jewelry, she'd be wearing almost nothing at all."

As tempted as I was to dish the dirt with Mary, my rumbling stomach reminded me that like a certain pudgy pooch, it was waiting to be fed.

Before hanging up, I thanked Mary for being such a good friend and I promised to be at the Semple manse bright and early with a supply of the Koffee Kabin's best coffee and freshest doughnuts.

I then phoned Milano's and placed an order for a large, thin-crust pizza with extra cheese and sausage. The kid who took the order said he would see to it that my pizza would be delivered extra fast. Pesty, who'd been listening, immediately stopped devouring the Dandy Diet dog food that I had carefully measured out and placed in her food bowl.

"Like my mother used to say, if you finish what you start, you might be surprised at what you find," I lectured to the little Kees. I was of course referring to the half-eaten dog food and the soon-to-be-delivered pizza. At the time I thought the words fit the situation rather nicely. I never suspected that I would soon find an even better fit for my mother's prophetic saying and there would be nothing nice about it.

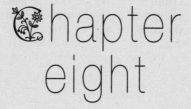

Chapter
eight

The following morning I was up and dressed with plenty
of time to stop at the Koffee Kabin, get the promised
treats, and be at the Semple place before Mary and Herbie
showed up with the goods. Because the weather forecast
included the continuation of record heat and humidity, I'd
decided to wear my olive drab camp shirt with matching
shorts and sneakers. Not wanting to fuss with my hair, I
swept it into a tight topknot and secured the practical do
with a red scrunchy. I then tiptoed out of the master bedroom and crept down the stairs, taking care not to disturb
the sleeping Charlie and Pesty.

As I walked past the hall mirror, I was startled by the
sight of my own image. Staring back at me was someone
who looked like a giant olive in search of a martini. I considered ditching the entire outfit but in an effort to stay on
time and on track, I traded the more fashionable topknot
for a droopy ponytail and the red scrunchy for a plain,
brown rubber band. Within twenty minutes of leaving Kettle Cottage, I was sharing fresh coffee and doughnuts with

Mary and Herbie in the cozy confines of the old Victorian's new front porch.

Faster than it took Biddy McFarland to get her gardening tools and station herself in the nearby shrubbery, Herbie, with help from Mary and me, had the truck unloaded. He was nice enough to move some of the heavier items to the appropriate areas before heading back to England's Fine Furniture.

Since it was my intention to subtly bring attention to functional space and future possibilities for its use, it didn't take long to get the house staged. I was especially pleased with how the kitchen-dinette area turned out. The round, glass-topped, wrought-iron bistro table with two matching chairs would draw people into the area where they would notice the bay window with its custom-built window seat that offered additional hidden storage. The colorful accent pillows that I'd added gave the entire kitchen area a cozy feeling that invited usage.

By lunchtime I was satisfied that I'd done my best. The old manse was ready for Amanda Little's Saturday evening sneak peek and Sunday's all-important open house.

After carefully locking up, I gave Mary a hug of gratitude for all her help, and with a wave to the ever-watchful Biddy McFarland, Mary and I hopped in my van and headed for the country club, a well-deserved meal, and a glass of wine.

With no valet on duty, I dropped Mary off at the front door and went in search of a parking space. Between the glut of golfers out on the course and the usual lunch-hour crowd, I ended up parking in the last row that was separated from the eighteenth fairway by a thick clump of tall bushes. I'd just gotten out of the van when the sound of a vaguely familiar male voice drifted over the tall hedge. It only took me a moment to match a face with the voice of the not very happy golfer—Ben Kind.

"Listen to me and listen good," he snarled, "unlike you, I have to live in this town. I took enough flak from our

winning the golf tournament thanks to your creative score
keeping, and I'm not about to have what's left of my reputation get destroyed by any more of your shenanigans.
Duke Demarco is nobody to mess with, and like the Hastings woman, he expects to be paid." Ben Kind's anger
was palpable. "Maybe if you'd controlled your gambling
habit and kept your sticky fingers in your own pocket, you
wouldn't be in a cash bind. I'm warning you, Stuart, get
your act together or else."

Any response or explanation that Stuart Goodenough
had to offer was lost in the sound of the golf cart's motor as
it resumed its trek down the narrow fairway. Reacting to
the warning cry of "fore," I automatically ducked, thus
narrowly avoided being struck in the head by a fast moving
golf ball. I didn't wait around to confront its owner. Instead, I hurriedly made my way out of the parking lot and
into the clubhouse where Mary was comfortably ensconced
in the bar and grill's oversized back booth.

With smoking allowed in this informal dining area, I
gratefully lit a cigarette and took a large sip of the excellent Webber's Bay Chardonnay that the thoughtful Mary
had waiting for me.

"My stars, Gin, you should really think about giving up
smoking. Your hands are shaking and you're short of
breath. If I didn't know any better, I'd almost guess that
someone or something scared the daylights out of you. I do
wish you would try the patch. It worked for me and I know
it could work for you."

I figured it was a lot easier to blame my behavior on the
demon tobacco than try to explain my experience in the
parking lot. Eventually, Mary's ongoing pitch for the patch
was interrupted by the appearance of Harry and Bambi
Eastwood. For a frightening moment, I thought they were
going to join us, but at the last minute, the much bejeweled
Bambi dragged Harry into the bar.

By the time Mary and I had finished our lunch, Stuart
Goodenough had made his way into the bar without so
much as a wave or nod in my direction. But for the pres-

ence of Biddy and Gordy McFarland (they'd been seated at a table in the middle of the room where they could observe everything and everybody), I would have taken the opportunity to inform Stuart and his fellow flippers that Designer Jeans had completed its part of the flip project and expected to be paid the balance owed as promised.

On our way home from the country club, Mary and I stopped by the bungalow on Tall Timber Road for a visit with JR, baby Kris, and the ailing Matt. Some thirty minutes later, I dropped Mary off at England's Fine Furniture and headed for Kettle Cottage. Thanks to Mary's offer to babysit Matt and the three kids, JR would be on hand for Amanda Little's Saturday evening visit to the staged house. I was looking forward to my daughter's company almost as much as she was looking forward to the break from Matt and the frequent ringing of the porcelain bell.

All things considered, such as having to listen to Herbie Waddlemeyer's latest alien encounter, staging the old house, the parking lot incident, Mary's lecture on the benefits of the patch, and the short but pleasant visit with JR and Co., it had been a pretty full day.

Chapter nine

By five thirty Saturday evening, I'd fixed Charlie a quick meal of hot dogs and beans (obviously the man didn't marry me for my culinary skills) and filled Pesty's bowl with a carefully measured amount of Dandy Diet dog food. By six o'clock I was ready and waiting for the perpetually late JR. I breathed a sigh of relief when less than ten minutes after the hour, the red pickup truck with JR at the wheel arrived at Kettle Cottage.

Even though the ride to the Semple house was a relatively short one, it was long enough for me to tell my daughter about Friday's parking lot incident, something I deliberately hadn't mentioned to neither Mary nor Charlie.

"Why," said JR after I related Ben Kind's side of the conversation I'd overheard, "am I not surprised. You know, Mom, when you think about it, what do we really know about Stuart Goodenough or for that matter, the Eastwoods. Mr. Eastwood seems like a nice enough guy but like Grandma Kelly would say, the evil that men do is more often than not hidden behind a kind face and winning smile. Have you given any thought about asking Horatio to do a background check on the Eastwoods and Mr. Goodenough?"

JR was referring to Horatio Bordeaux, a close friend of mine who, because of medical problems, had given up a promising career with the Central Intelligence Agency and returned to Seville, where he started his own business on the Web. He specializes in locating hard-to-find people, places, and information. The rotund, wheelchair-bound diabetic is always discreet and has more connections than a Tammany Hall politician.

"That's something I should have done before I committed Designer Jeans to the flip project. To be honest with you, JR, I'd be too embarrassed to go to him now," I admitted before adding, "besides, I'm not all that anxious to do battle with Mrs. Daggert, Horatio's housekeeper from hell. Did I ever tell you about the time she threatened to put a curse on me just because I wouldn't tell her why I needed to see her boss?"

"Only about thirty thousand times. Honestly, Mother, you're the only person who has trouble with the dear old soul," JR said, easing the truck into a parking spot three houses down from the Semple manse.

We both waved to Biddy and her mother, Vilma, as we made our way over to the silver Lexus parked nearby where Amanda Little was patiently awaiting our arrival. Even though we didn't actually see the nosy (albeit neighborly) women, we could feel their eyes watching our every move.

The clock in the town square marked the quarter hour as the real estate agent emerged from the luxury auto. Dressed in her trademark white and gold, the fair Amanda seemed to shimmer in the fading sunlight. My sincere apology for being late was lost in her enthusiastic greeting.

Even though the calendar hadn't officially proclaimed the end of summer, the early evening air was fall-like in its chill. Since Amanda, along with everyone else involved in the flip, had a key for the house, I was puzzled that she had waited for us in her car rather than inside the old Victorian. The puzzle was solved when we reached the front door of the Semple house.

"Oh good," remarked Amanda, sounding relieved when I fished the house key with its distinctive Designer Jeans tag from the bottom of my overstuffed leather purse, "you've got your key. I've either lost or misplaced mine, something I'm not about to admit to the Fast Flippers. I hope I find it before tomorrow's open house. It's on my favorite key chain, the one the chamber of commerce gave me last year. It has my initials on it in solid gold."

"I'm sure it'll turn up soon. In the meantime, you can use my key. If I'm right about the staging job, Designer Jeans's part of the project is finished," I said, sticking the key into the lock and giving it a turn. "The only thing left for me to do is to collect the balance of the money owed to Designer Jeans at tomorrow's open house and I don't need a key for that."

"That may be so but if I'm right about Stuart, you're going to have to stand in line for your money, right behind Duke Demarco," said the petite Amanda, stepping over the threshold and into the house. If she had more to say about Stuart Goodenough, she apparently put the subject on hold for the time being.

Amanda's gold designer shoes with the pointy toes and high heels tapped smartly over the recently refurbished hardwood floors. Clad in jeans, sweatshirts, and Reeboks, JR and I quietly padded after her. Unlike the fashion-conscious Amanda, we were not dressed to kill.

The profusion of praise the real estate agent had for the staging project fed my ego and strengthened my resolve to collect every penny owed Designer Jeans for a job well done. I was about to ask Amanda to be more specific about her being "right" regarding Stuart Goodenough when she caught sight of the kitchen-dinette area with its bistro table and window seat.

"Merciful heavens! If this doesn't sell the place," proclaimed the awestruck Amanda Little, "I'm going to turn in my real estate license and get into a different line of work. You know, when you first proposed putting in a window seat, I thought it sounded rather nice but I had no idea it would become the focal point of the entire area. Talk about warm and welcoming. It fairly shouts 'make yourself at home,' which is the secret to selling a house."

Because the window seat had been more JR's idea than mine, I was eager to see my daughter's reaction to the accent pillows I'd added to the piece the previous day. But to my dismay, I noticed that something was different. A pillow was missing. It was the distinctive mauve-colored one that was embroidered with the message: REST IN PEACE. I had debated with Mary about using the pillow with its portentous message. She thought it was cute while I thought it was creepy. Since I had rejected all of Mary's other decor suggestions, I reluctantly gave in and tucked the puffy pillow between two larger and, in my opinion, more suitable ones.

Now the pillow in question was gone. Being that it was an inanimate object, I knew it hadn't disappeared under its own power. Somebody had removed it. But who and why? Maybe, I reasoned silently, Mary decided I was right after all and had placed the pillow inside the window seat while I was busy staging another area and had simply forgotten to mention it. That seemed to be the most logical explanation for the missing item so I wasn't exactly surprised when JR lifted the lid of the seat and let out a gasp. But I was definitely surprised by what happened next.

"Holy crap," JR exclaimed at the top of her voice, allowing the lid of the seat to slam down with such force that the pillows on it scattered into a jumbled heap, "that's the most hideous thing I've ever seen in my entire life! Who could have done such a thing?"

"I kinda figure it was either Mary or maybe even Herbie Waddlemeyer," I said as I attempted to restore order to the window seat pillows. "They both had the opportunity and were aware of how I felt about the matter. If it makes you feel any better, I agree with you about it being hideous." I didn't bother to add that I thought she was overreacting. At least I thought she was until I opened the lid of the window seat and peered inside of it.

What followed was like something straight out of the 1944 Warner Brothers outrageous dark comedy, the classic *Arsenic and Old Lace*.

"Jesus, Mary, and Joseph," I screeched, jumping back and knocking JR off balance, something that sent her careening into the arms of a bewildered Amanda. Like JR, I, too, let the lid of the window seat slam down with a resounding thud. "There's something in the window seat besides an ugly pillow and it's not moving!"

"What in the world are you two bellowing about?" Amanda Little coolly demanded as she extracted herself from JR's grasp. Without waiting for the answer, she marched over to the seat, opened the lid, picked up the mauve-colored pillow and did a classic double take. "Oh my God," she screamed, "it's Stuart Goodenough! I think he's dead and I think I'm going to be sick. Forget the open house. It's toast."

Sunday's open house had become Saturday night's crime scene. The golden girl of Seville's chamber of commerce was right on all counts.

Chapter
ten

"Is she okay?" I inquired when JR returned to the kitchen area after being sure Amanda had made it safely to the nearest bathroom.

"Yeah. I think she's more embarrassed than anything else. Fortunately, her aim was good. Other than messing up her lipstick a bit, she seems to be fine. I told her to take her time and to holler if she needs help," JR replied, pulling up a bar stool and sitting down at the kitchen island.

"Listen, JR," I said, dumping the contents of my purse across the island's speckled beige-and-black quartz composite top in an effort to find my cell phone, "forget what I said about Mary or Herbie being responsible for the window seat business. At the time I said that, I thought we were talking about that stupid pillow."

"Good lord, Mom, I'm not exactly an idiot. If you recall, I was the first one to look inside the window seat. No way in hell did I think for even one second that Aunt Mary or Mr. Waddlemeyer had anything to do with what I saw. Neither one of them would hurt a fly and they certainly wouldn't murder anyone, and I do think he was murdered."

"And I certainly agree," Amanda Little said as she entered the kitchen and joined us at the island. Other than looking a bit on the pale side, the beautiful real estate agent had pulled herself together and was ready for my announcement that I was going to telephone the police.

The 911 call was taken by Officer Jasper Merkle, a rookie on the Seville police force. Once I convinced the skinny, perpetually nervous Jasper that I wasn't some crackpot making a false report, he instructed me to stay put and not to touch or move anything, including the victim.

"Never fear," he said, before hanging up, "help is on the way."

"Ten-four," I shot back, snapping the cell phone shut and returning it to my purse.

"Let me guess," said JR with a smile, "Officer Merkle handled the call. Am I right?"

"It was either him or Mayberry's Barney Fife," I quipped, making reference to the TV character portrayed to the hilt by Don Knotts. "Unfortunately, Jasper Merkle is a real person and not the product of some comedy writer's imagination."

"Jasper is no better or worse than Rollie Stevens," Amanda Little said before adding, "Arthur Kraft told me that if the town council hadn't been so insistent about having the chief sign that contract, they could have forced him into retirement five years ago. Instead, the contract gives him the job until he decides to call it quits."

"Or dies," added JR, "and that's something nobody hopes will happen anytime soon. Not even Matt."

With his head of white, wooly hair, raisin-like eyes, rosy red lips, and light brown skin, the chubby lawman looks more like a gingerbread cookie than Seville top cop. Although he seems to care more about protecting the environment and the rights of animals than protecting the citizens of Seville, Rollie Stevens is a good man and nobody's fool. In spite of having to handle the bulk of the chief's workload, my son-in-law has seen to it that everyone on and off the force treats Chief Stevens with respect. I was about to bring this to Amanda's attention when the sound of sirens signaled the approach of emergency vehicles.

Unlike Biddy McFarland, I didn't rush to the window in an effort to share in the excitement of the moment. It wasn't necessary since once again I'd managed to entangle Designer Jeans in a murder, something that I knew I would have to explain sooner or later to my police lieutenant son-in-law.

Matt never misses an opportunity to remind me that he is a cop and I'm not. I am to keep my nose out of his business and he'll keep his nose out of mine . . . blah, blah, blah. My failure to do so on a couple of occasions in the past has been the only wrinkle in an otherwise relatively smooth relationship. I also knew I would have to tell Charlie, who has always sided with Matt in regard to my steering clear of police business, that once again I was involved in a real-life murder mystery.

Maybe this time I'll play by Matt's rules, I said to myself. "Or maybe not," I said aloud as JR, responding to the pounding on the front door, ushered Police Chief Stevens, Officer Patti Crump, and the ambulance crew into the house.

JR returned to the kitchen to find me leaning against the counter with my eyes closed and my lips moving.

"Mother," hissed JR, "what in God's name are you muttering about?"

"I was not muttering," I said, opening my eyes and coming to my own defense, "I was sending an emergency SOS to St. Blaise."

"I'll probably regret asking but I'll do it anyway. Why an SOS and why him?" Like her father, JR tends to be skeptical when it comes to heavenly intervention.

"Because," I retorted, "I've got a funny feeling that before this whole murder business is over, we are going to need a lot of help. You know, the kind that only Matt and his sidekick, Sergeant Sid Rosen, can provide so I thought I'd better contact St. Blaise."

"Ohhkaay," replied JR, stretching out the word, "and he's the patron saint of what? Homicide investigations?"

"Of course not," I said, ignoring the sarcasm that had crept into her voice. "He's the patron saint of sore throats. Maybe he can use his saintly influence and speed up Matt's recovery."

"While you're praying," said Amanda Little, who'd been listening to the mother/daughter good-natured bantering, "perhaps you could put in a word for me. I've got a sinking feeling that when all is said and done, I'm going to be arrested for Stuart Goodenough's murder."

Having said that, the beautiful Amanda announced in a voice loud enough to be heard by everyone that she was going to be sick again and took off running for the nearest bathroom.

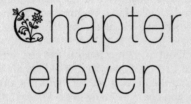

Chapter eleven

The ambulance crew made several attempts to resuscitate Stuart Goodenough, but it was obvious that the man was beyond help. Even though the cause of death had yet to be officially determined, based on comments made by the crew regarding the red dots they observed on the inside of the dead man's eyelids, I was willing to bet that the pillow in the window seat had played a significant role in Stuart Goodenough's death.

Despite what she'd said about being arrested for the deed, I couldn't see how the petite Amanda would have had the strength to overpower someone the size of the real estate broker turned entrepreneur, much less stuff his body in the window seat. Granted, Stuart wasn't a large man but he was solidly built, like a welterweight boxer, while Amanda probably weighed less than a certain not-so-little Keeshond.

Officer Crump, following the police chief's instructions, escorted JR and me into the living room area where we were told to remain for the time being. We made ourselves comfortable in the love seat I'd positioned near the massive fireplace. A pair of brass-and-glass wall sconces (original to the house) provided a minimum of light, leaving the framed portrait above the fireplace's marble mantel bathed in shadows. I'd almost decided not to use the oil painting, which I had discovered in a battered wardrobe cabinet that was beyond saving, but at the last minute I changed my mind.

Feeling about as melancholy as the girl in the painting, I asked Patti Crump if Amanda would be joining us.

"I wouldn't count on it seeing that she's already identified the key and chain as being hers. The fact that they was found in the window seat along with the victim don't look all that good for Miz Little. She claims that she lost or misplaced it but she don't remember where or when."

"Hey, Patti," Dr. Sue Lin Loo, the attractive, exotic-looking, capable medical examiner called out as she peeked into the living room area, "the chief wants you to get that yellow tape up ASAP. I had to practically push Biddy McFarland and some old lady in a souped-up scooter off the brick sidewalk in order to reach the front porch."

Until Loo made her findings official, the cause of death in this case would remain undetermined, but I was willing to bet that the real estate broker had been asphyxiated. I was also willing to bet that someone other than Amanda Little held the mauve-colored pillow over Stuart's face. How to prove this seemed as daunting a task as painting with a worn-out brush. It can be done but the end result may be a disappointment.

After what seemed like a lifetime of waiting, Officer Crump returned and took our statements. When that had been accomplished, Chief Stevens announced that JR and I were free to leave. I was about to ask him how Amanda Little was holding up when a noisy dispute erupted at the front door of the old Victorian. Hilly R. Murrow, Seville's leading (and only) print and radio reporter had arrived.

Not wanting to be scooped by the likes of Biddy McFarland, the hawk-faced, keen-eyed Hilly tried her best to get past the formidable Patti Crump. Failing that, and waving her ever-present notebook and pencil, Hilly demanded that the chief provide her with all the gory details of what had transpired in the kitchen-dinette area.

"Come on, JR," I cried, grabbing my purse with one hand and my daughter's arm with the other. "If we hurry, we can get out the back door and be in your truck before Hilly spots us."

"Who cares if she sees us or not, Mom. It's not like we're suspects in a murder. The only thing we're guilty of is finding a dead body in the window seat. It's truly a matter of being in the wrong place at the wrong time."

"Yeah? I'll bet poor Amanda Little feels the same way as you do and it's not helping her at all. Besides, I think it would be a lot better for us if things were explained to our husbands before, rather than after, they read Hilly Murrow's cockeyed version of events, which I'm sure will be splashed all over the front page of the *Seville Sentinel*."

"Oh rats, I forgot all about Matt and Pops," said JR. Her lovely face looked more mischievous than worried as she followed me down the hall and out the back door. "I don't envy your having to tell them that not only have you once again gotten involved in a murder but dragged me into it, too. Good luck, especially with Matt."

"Let me put it to you this way, my darling daughter, if I have to face those two guys all by my lonesome, you can drop me at the nearest airport and tell your children that Grandma's joined the peace corps."

"Mother." JR giggled as we reached the safety of her truck. "I was only teasing. You break the news to Pops and I'll take care of telling Matt. Once that's out of the way, I'll meet you at the airport. Maybe with a little luck, the peace corps will send us to Outer Mongolia. I hear it's beautiful this time of the year."

The sound of the pickup truck's motor, along with our unrestrained laughter, drowned out the sound of Hilly Murrow's grating voice ordering us to halt as we drove away from the scene of Seville's latest homicide.

Upon arriving home, I found Charlie in the den, where he was apparently sleeping off the effects of a double helping of Ben & Jerry's ice cream flavor of the month. With Pesty collapsed at her master's feet and lacking the energy to greet me, I strongly suspected that the roly-poly ball of fur had been given more than a puppy portion of the calorie-laden treat.

Deciding to adhere to the old adage of not disturbing sleeping dogs, I was about to beat a hasty retreat to the master bathroom and a hot shower when the sound of my husband's voice stopped me in my tracks.

"Well, well. Look who's home. It's Seville's answer to Agatha Christie's Herkimer Parrot."

Although Charlie had fractured the fictional detective's name, I thought it best not to bring it to his attention. Instead, I steeled myself for the now-familiar lecture and wondered how he knew about my involvement in yet another untimely and unexpected death.

"So who's the lucky—no, change that to the unlucky— stiff this time? I hope it isn't anyone I know. And while your little gray cells are busy searching for that answer, maybe you can explain to me why you had to drag our daughter into the latest murder mess. I'm sure a certain police lieutenant is wondering the same thing."

"Hilly Murrow," I said through clenched teeth as I figured out my husband's source, "Jeez, I should have known she'd call the house. I suppose it's too late to warn JR."

"You got that right, sweetheart. When that goofy dame discovered that I didn't know what she was yammering about, she damn near broke my eardrum slamming down the phone. I figured I'd better get to Matt before she did but I was too late. The line was busy. So I called Rollie Stevens and he gave me the whole story."

Getting up from his favorite chair, a well-worn, brown chenille-covered recliner, Charlie suggested that I tell him my version of events over a pot of hot cocoa.

Neither one of us had much to say about anything as I moved about the kitchen preparing the hot drink. Reaching into the pantry cabinet, I removed my private stash of JR's homemade shortbread cookies.

When I presented Charlie with a steaming mug of hot cocoa, topped with a hefty dollop of whipped cream and accompanied by a tall stack of the buttery pastries, the smile on my husband's face told me I was home free and all was forgiven. I could only hope that JR fared as well since neither one of us had the wardrobe or wherewithal necessary to survive in Genghis Khan's homeland, peace corps or no peace corps.

Chapter twelve

The next morning, Charlie downed his standard quick breakfast of orange juice, toast, and coffee before leaving Kettle Cottage for his Sunday morning golf match with his partner and brother-in-law, Denny England. With Charlie out of the house and Pesty engaged in scouring the kitchen floor for tidbits of toast, I reached for the Mickey Mouse phone and punched the cartoon character's buttons.

Despite the early hour, JR answered the call on the first ring. From the background noise, it was clear to me that my daughter's Sunday had begun with the usual flurry of activities.

Shouting to be heard over the bickering twins, barking dog, and the demanding cries of a hungry baby, JR informed me that she would call me back after seeing Matt off to work.

"Wow! That St. Blaise doesn't fool around. Too bad I didn't think of him sooner," I said to the preoccupied Pesty.

Surrendering the phone to the waiting arms of the oversized Disney icon with the changeling smile, I wondered how Charlie felt about re-gifting. "Trust me, pal," I informed Walt's rascally rodent, "one way or another, your days as my kitchen phone are numbered."

Three cups of coffee and a cigarette later, JR called me back. Both Mickey and I were all ears.

"To begin with," JR said, "Aunt Mary was the one who answered the phone when Hilly Murrow was trying to touch base with Matt last night. What happened was that the more Hilly carried on, the more she managed to confuse Aunt Mary.

"When she finally was able to get a word in, Aunt Mary told Hilly in no uncertain terms that the idea of the two of us fleeing a crime scene on an elderly woman's motor scooter was absolutely preposterous. Before hanging up on her, Aunt Mary suggested Hilly take two aspirins, get a good night's sleep, and call Rollie Stevens in the morning.

"Aunt Mary tried to repeat the conversation to Matt but that only led to further confusion. By the time I got home, they were both ready and eager to hear my side of the story."

"And how did Matt react?" I asked with my heart in my mouth. "Did he carry on about my keeping my nose out of police business? You know, the usual tirade."

"Not really," said JR, "in fact, he was relieved that we were both safe and not charged with anything, including murder or obstruction of justice. When he kissed me and the kids good-bye this morning, he was in a pretty good mood."

"And in pretty good health, thanks to St. Blaise. Now maybe you won't be such a doubting Thomas like someone else we both know and love," I said, making what I thought was a clever reference to her "I'll believe it when I see it" father. But JR was having none of it.

"I hate to burst your celestial bubble, Mom, but Matt's seemingly sudden return to good health was the result of the medicine that Doc Parker prescribed finally kicking in. And while we're on the subject of mini-miracles, tell Aunt Mary that the hot lemonade she practically forced Matt to drink didn't cure him, either. It only made him sleepy and thirsty. Hey, I gotta go. I've got three kids, a dog, and a cat, plus a couple of birds and gerbils all waiting to be fed. If I find out anything new about the murder investigation, I'll let you know. Love ya."

"I love you, too," I replied but JR had already hung up. Unlike my daughter, the only thing that I needed to feed was my insatiable appetite for solving puzzles, especially murderous ones.

"The best place to start," I said to a disinterested Pesty and sounding like a character out of Lewis Carroll's *Alice's Adventures in Wonderland*, "is at the beginning, something I should have done before getting Designer Jeans involved with the Fast Flippers and this whole house-flipping business."

Luck was on my side when Horatio, and not the dreaded Mrs. Daggert, answered the phone. Before I had a chance to say hello, my old friend greeted me by name and with a question.

"Jeannie, what took you so long?" he asked, "I've been sitting by the phone waiting for your call."

"If that's true, then I assume you've read about my latest foray into Homicide 101," I replied in an effort to keep things light in case Mrs. Daggert was hovering in the background.

"No, no," protested Horatio with a deep chuckle, "I haven't the slightest interest in fiction. That seems to be Hilly Murrow's forte. Besides, I've always found Mrs. Daggert's ability to sense when something's not quite right to be much more reliable than anything I've read in the *Sentinel*, which is why I've been waiting for your call."

"Mrs. Daggert? What in the world has she been saying about me now?" I didn't bother to hide my surprise or irritation.

"Now, Jeannie, don't get on your high horse. Mrs. Daggert became concerned upon hearing that Designer Jeans was involved in the Semple project. She's convinced the old house is rife with evil spirits. She predicted that you'd be seeking my help. The only part she apparently got wrong was that she thought you would contact me sooner rather than later. So tell me, Jeannie, what can I do for you?"

I was sorely tempted to fib (something I've been known to do on rare occasions) and inform Horatio that my call was strictly a social one. That would have really put a crimp in the wickedly wacky housekeeper's prediction. Instead, I was honest with Horatio, who, after listening to the whole sordid mess I'd gotten Designer Jeans into, agreed to meet with me in his home office.

"Great," I said, "I'll stop by on my way back from twelve o'clock mass at St. Brendan's."

"Egads! Either I heard you wrong about going to church or it's some holy day I'm not aware of," said Horatio, feigning shock.

Resisting the opportunity to exchange witticisms with the most intelligent person I've ever known, I wished him a holy Sunday and ended the call. If I hurried, I could shower, dress, put on some makeup, fix my hair and be on time for mass.

With the prospect of having to deal with Mrs. Daggert, the thought of sitting through one of Father Murphy's lengthy sermons and enduring a lot of off-key hymn singing (thanks to a tone-deaf choir director) didn't seem all that bad.

I'd decided that my attendance at Sunday mass would provide me with an opportunity to go directly to the top with my latest request for heavenly help, something I knew would be needed the minute I saw the Sunday edition of the *Sentinel* with its sensational headline—Ms. Little in Big Trouble! If nothing else, Hilly Murrow has a way with words.

According to the reporter's front-page article, the beautiful, three-time winner of Seville's chamber of commerce award and real estate agent extraordinaire would soon be sporting a jumpsuit of jailhouse orange and a pair of plastic flip-flops, courtesy of the county prosecutor.

Chapter thirteen

The parking lot at St. Brendan's is as small as the church building is large. I ended up parking the van in the driveway of the rectory. Seeing that it was Sunday, I reasoned correctly that Father Murphy wouldn't be going anywhere for a while, at least not until twelve o'clock mass was over.

In an effort to attract as little attention as possible, I slipped into church through an open side door. Spotting Mary in the crowd, I tiptoed my way across the aisle to where she was sitting. Using my hand, I motioned to her to slide over.

"My stars, what a surprise seeing you here and it's not even Easter or Christmas," exclaimed Mary in an Irish whisper that could be heard all the way from St. Brendan's to the Emerald Isle and back again without losing so much as a single syllable.

"Very funny, Mar," I whispered, pushing my way into the pew. I was about to treat my best friend and Charlie's twin sister to one of my signature sharp retorts when Father Murphy, accompanied by two teenage altar boys with Mohawk haircuts and nose rings, strode down the center aisle on their way to the front of the church. Mass was about to begin. My blistering comeback would have to wait.

Between the kneeling, standing, sitting, off-key singing, and Father Murphy's sermon, I actually managed to squeeze in some heavy-duty, private praying. By the time the good padre announced that we should go in peace (the signal that the mass was over), I decided to follow his advice and gave Mary a forgiving pat on the arm as we slipped out the side door of the church. I'd also decided to ask Mary to accompany me to Horatio's.

"Honestly, Gin," said Mary, "you are just full of surprises. Last night you were at a crime scene, today you show up at church, and now you want me to go sleuthing with you."

"Listen, Mar, you've got about half a second to give me an answer, otherwise I'm going solo to Horatio's. If I'm not back before the sun goes down, check with Mrs. Daggert. She's bound to have the answer to what happened to me. I'm assuming that you would be at least mildly interested in my well-being." I was back to being my old, hard self despite having spent nearly an hour basking in religious fervor. It felt great.

"Of course I'll go with you to Horatio's, Gin. If nothing else, it will be a chance for me to visit with Mrs. Daggert. You know, the lotion she gave me for my chapped hands really did the trick."

"Dear God, I can't believe you actually used some of that smelly goop she keeps in one of those little bottles she's always waving at me. She has a supply of them hooked on that chain she wears around her waist." I raised my arms up in the air, a universal signal of surrender. "You're a better man than I am, Gunga Din," I said, borrowing a line from the works of Rudyard Kipling, the famous British writer.

"Huh?" was Mary's reply. I was about to explain the reference when I caught sight of Hilly Murrow. Striding across the sidewalk toward the driveway, the reporter was within hailing distance when I shoved Mary (who had walked to church) into the van and drove off, leaving Hilly sputtering in the dust. Ten minutes and a series of tricky turns later, we arrived at Horatio's house.

"Good," I said, parking the van and unbuckling my seat belt, "nobody followed us or if they did, I lost them."

"My stars, you almost lost me on that last turn," declared a disheveled Mary as she struggled to get out of the van. "Maybe Matt's right about leaving the detective stuff to the police. I hope Mrs. Daggert has something to settle my nerves and tummy. Some peppermint tea would be nice."

Mary had barely gotten the words out about the tea when the front door of the house flew open and there stood Mrs. Daggert in her gypsy finery, chain belt and all. Dressed from head to toe in a shimmering purple frock and looking like something a black cat had dragged in, the old crone of a housekeeper greeted Mary with a hug and me with a scowl.

"Come in, my dear," she said sweetly to Mary while leaving me on my own. "I've got a pot of peppermint tea brewing in the kitchen. I'm sure you would appreciate a cup about now. The peppermint will settle your nerves as well as your stomach."

"Excuse me, Mrs. Daggert, but do you think you could tell your boss that I'm here?" I said, somehow managing to keep my temper under control. I didn't bother to mention that it would have been nice if she'd offered me some tea or better yet, a cup of fresh, hot coffee.

"I already told him you're here, Mrs. Hastings. Mr. Bordeaux is waiting for you in his office," she croaked, waving her gnarled fingers at the closed double doors off the foyer. "I put an extra mug on the tray along with the flask of coffee I made earlier today. You'll find what you're looking for in the master's office."

"She's something else, isn't she?" Mary said to me before disappearing into the kitchen with the housekeeper-cum-hostess.

"She certainly is," said Horatio, sliding the pocket doors open and welcoming me into his private office, "that and much, much more. Wouldn't you agree, Jeannie?"

"I won't argue with you about that," I said with a tight smile before steering the conversation to the reason for my visit. I quickly filled him in on everything I knew about the flipping of the old Victorian, starting with Amanda Little's phone call with her almost-too-good-to-be-true offer and ending with the almost-too-hard-to-believe murder of Stuart Goodenough. I also told him about everything in between, including my failure to contact him earlier to do a background check on the smooth-talking Stuart; the seemingly meek and mild Harry Eastwood; and Bambi Eastwood, a living, breathing Barbie doll with the brains to match.

A couple of hours later, and with the promise that he would proceed at top speed to get me the information I should have requested before getting involved with the Fast Flippers, our visit had come to an end.

"Now, Jeannie, promise me that you'll stay out of trouble, at least until I've got something to report. Maybe by then you'll know more about whom you're dealing with before going off half-cocked."

Even though Horatio's words were delivered in a light-hearted manner, I knew my old friend well enough to see the concern in his eyes.

"Oh, and another thing," said Horatio with a sly grin, "to make sure that we leave no stone unturned, so to speak, I'm also going to do a little checking on Seville's own."

"Who do you have in mind?" I asked, thinking he was going to mention Ben Kind's name, which wouldn't have surprised me all that much. But when he rattled off Ben's name, along with that of Duke Demarco, Amanda Little, and Arthur Kraft I was left speechless. Or almost.

"You've got to be kidding," I sputtered, "especially Arthur Kraft. He doesn't have anything to do with the Fast Flippers, unless you count the crush he has on Amanda Little. Interesting. Perhaps the bashful Arthur is a closet psycho and decided to 'off' the competition. Hmm, I hadn't thought of that. You know, Horatio, you've got the makings of a detective and a damn good one at that."

"No way. That's more your forte than mine. I'm the gatherer of information, which I give to others to use wisely. Now, get out of here so I can get to work. I'll be in touch. In the meantime, Jeannie, please try to stay out of trouble."

Once Mary and I had said good-bye to my friend Horatio and to Mary's friend Mrs. Daggert, we got in the van and began the short ride to the England residence. While I did the driving, Mary did the talking, most of which centered on the housekeeper's supposed phenomenal abilities.

"Do you think Mrs. Daggert is psychic?" asked Mary. Her blue eyes were open wide, giving her the appearance of a wondering adolescent.

"No, I don't. I think the woman's more psycho than psychic. But I do think that she's a good guesser," I said in an attempt to put an end to the subject, which it did. By the time I dropped Mary off at her home, she was more concerned that we'd skipped lunch than whether or not Mrs. Daggert had a crystal ball rolling around somewhere in her knobby little head.

Chapter fourteen

✺

Monday dawned dark and dreary with enough cloud cover to convince even the most optimistic forecaster that central Indiana was in for a day of persistent rain showers.

While Charlie caught up on the national news via CNN, I only glanced at Hilly Murrow's latest article in the *Sentinel* regarding Stuart Goodenough's murder. It seemed to be a rehash of the previous day's article and not worth reading. I was about to toss the paper aside when the words "something's rotten in real estate land" caught my eye. The more I read, the angrier I became. Without so much as a smidgen of evidence, Hilly Murrow hinted strongly that perhaps the charismatic Stuart and the lovely-to-look-at Amanda had a falling out over the sharing of monies skimmed from funds earmarked to cover expenses incurred during the flip process.

While I ranted and raved about Hilly Murrow's foray into yellow journalism and McCarthyism, Charlie quietly deposited the newspaper in the recycle bin, poured us both a second cup of coffee, and announced that it was the perfect day to clean out the cellar. Since he'd come to the

breakfast table dressed in a pair of well-worn Levi's and a
sweatshirt that had seen better days, I knew he was serious. I also knew that as far as he was concerned, the subject of Stuart Goodenough's murder was closed.

"Jeez, I don't envy you. That's one job I wouldn't want
to tackle even if you paid me," I said in an effort to insure
that my own plans for the day didn't include giving Charlie
a hand.

"Really? Sweetheart, if you thought that there was even
the slightest chance of solving some mystery or uncover-
ing evidence of a crime, you'd be down there searching
around like Pesty rooting for a treat."

I hate it when my husband is right. I had to do something
to balance the scales in my favor. "I beg to differ with you,
Charlie. Pesty, like all Keeshonds, has exceptionally good
manners. She would never stoop to rooting, nor would I." I
punctuated each sentence with puffs of smoke from my
newly lit cigarette. Joan Crawford, the screen actress who
practically invented the strong woman, would have been
impressed with how I handled the situation.

"Sez you. Watch this," Charlie said, gently placing half
a jelly doughnut in the dozing pooch's food bowl and covering the gooey pastry with a paper napkin.

With ears like a fox, the little Kees broke her own speed
record getting out from under the table and over to the
bowl where she tore away the napkin and scarfed down the
doughnut. Her black nose was coated in powdered sugar
when she resumed her morning nap.

"Thanks a lot, chum. Now you can clean up the mess,"
I grumbled, handing Charlie the broom and dustpan. "Did
anyone ever tell you that sometimes you are so juvenile?
I've better things to do with my time today than cleaning
up after you and the dog." I didn't mean to blurt out the last
sentence, which of course led to my husband's question.

"Such as?" said Charlie, using the dustpan to deliver a
playful swat to my backside. "It better not include sticking
that pretty nose of yours into Matt's business or you might
just find yourself in a cell instead of a cellar."

"For your information, chum," I replied, trying to come up with something other than the truth. "I've got clients to see, samples to show, and designs to finish. I'll probably be tied up for hours."

"Good girl. How about meeting me back here for dinner. You fix the food and I'll fix the drinks. And if you behave," teased Charlie, "I might even light a fire and watch the *Antiques Roadshow* with you."

"Hey, you're on. Make my drink a glass of Webber's Bay Chardonnay and I'll be yours for life," I told Charlie, giving him my best smile. "Any guy who willingly gives up watching *Monday Night Football* is my kind of man." Only much later did I find out the teams scheduled to play were two of my husband's least favorites.

Charlie returned my smile with a kiss before heading for the cellar and a full day's work. For some crazy, unfathomable reason, I wished him Godspeed.

"For chrissake, Jean, I'm going to the cellar, not outer space. I don't expect to run into anything more dangerous than a family of field mice or maybe a mole or two. You're the one who should be wished Godspeed. Trouble seems to follow you around even when you're not looking for it. So right back at you with the Godspeed thing. And shut the door, unless you want another mouse besides Mickey in the kitchen."

I quickly shut the door to the cellar and ran upstairs to the master bathroom, where I used my cell phone to place a fast call to Amanda Little to see if I could drop by. Feeling that the forty-something woman had had enough surprises lately, I didn't want to add yet another one by dropping in on her unexpectedly. I also wanted to be sure that she would be home. I had a lot of questions and felt that she could answer some of them. But would she do so was the biggest question of all.

The hinky feeling had returned and I had no intention of ignoring it, Matt or no Matt. In fact, I planned on checking with JR to find out if she'd managed to get any new information regarding the cause and time of death. From past experience, I knew that both would be crucial elements and would impact the investigation of the crime.

If time allowed, I also planned on visiting Biddy McFarland and her mother, Vilma. The two might have seen or heard something that seemed unimportant at the time and as such, they might not have mentioned it to anyone, not even Hilly Murrow. I didn't need intuition or psychic ability to know that by the end of the day, I would appreciate that glass of Chardonnay.

"Amanda Little at your service. At the moment I'm not able to come to the phone. Please leave a message and I will return your call as soon as possible. Thank you."

I hadn't expected a recorded message but with both the police and the press putting pressure on her to tell all and then some in an effort to directly tie her to Stuart Goodenough's death, I understood why the real estate agent was screening incoming phone calls. I was in the middle of leaving my own message when Amanda picked up the phone and cut in.

"Sorry about the message bit, Jean. As you've probably figured out by now there are certain people that I'd rather not speak to at the present time. You were saying something about dropping by this morning?"

"Yes, that is, if you feel up to it. I'll be honest with you, Amanda. I don't believe for one minute that you had anything to do with Stuart's death. I also don't believe Hilly Murrow's version of events. Her article in the *Sentinel* suggesting that you were a participant in Stuart's skimming scheme and that his death was the result of a falling out between thieves is ridiculous. If a murder wasn't involved, it would be laughable."

"Thanks for your faith in my innocence. So far, you and Arthur Kraft are on my short list of true friends," Amanda said, sounding close to tears.

"If JR's name isn't there, it should be. In fact, I've got this feeling that in the not-too-distant future your short list is going to take a giant growth spurt," I said in an effort to cheer up Amanda and shore up my own belief in her innocence.

The time we eventually settled on for my visit gave me less than a half hour to shower and dress. The showering part was fast and easy but finding something suitable to wear was not. As usual, I had more clothes in the laundry chute than in my closet. I finally settled on the same outfit I'd worn on Saturday night when we had discovered the body in the window seat. Slipping into the outfit, I wondered if it was possible for apparel to become an omen of bad luck.

"I hope not but I guess only time will tell," I said to Pesty as I checked myself over in the hall mirror.

Seeing that I had my purse slung over my left shoulder and the car keys in my right hand, a sign that I was about to leave the house, the appropriately named pooch whined her displeasure. Not sure if my fluffy four-legged friend wanted a parting pat or a parting treat, I played it safe and gave her both.

"You're going to have to depend on your master for lunch today," I advised the little Kees. "I've got places to go, things to do, and people to see." Closing both the top and bottom sections of the kitchen's Dutch door, I then splashed my way in the rain to my van parked on the side driveway.

The drive to Amanda Little's white clapboard and gold-colored trim, 1960s Dutch colonial house would be a short but wet one. The weather forecast calling for a full day of persistent showers was on the mark. Bad luck or not, in view of the inclement weather and being without an umbrella, I felt that I'd chosen the right outfit.

 Chapter
fifteen

"Come on in, Jean," cried Amanda Little, "before you end up soaking wet. Where's your umbrella?" she asked, peering around me as I stood on the front stoop that was inadequately covered by a small canopy. Because of its size, the canopy was strictly a decorative item and offered nothing in the line of protection from the elements.

The house was constructed at a time when practicality was often trumped by whatever was considered in vogue. In time, many once popular items such as fiberglass awnings, wrought-iron railings, hard-to-decipher house numbers, oversized flower boxes, and undersized canopies gave way to better and smarter architectural design elements.

"Amanda, if I knew where my umbrella was, I wouldn't be standing here with raindrops falling on my head, now would I?" I said with a laugh, taking care to avoid the growing puddle on the stoop as I stepped over the threshold and into the foyer. Expecting to be ushered into the real estate agent's living room/office, I was surprised to find that instead, I was being shown into what she referred to as the den.

"It used to be the formal dining room but I could count on one hand the times I used it for that purpose. Then one day it hit me—why not turn it into a den? Now that was something I both needed and wanted, so I did it," Amanda explained, opening the room's French doors and striking a pose. "Voila! My private sanctuary. You like?"

"You bet," I replied, relieved to see an absence of Amanda's preference for white with gold trim or gold with white trim. "You've followed one of the most important but often overlooked precepts of interior design. You've not only created an area that is as inviting as it is attractive but it is also useful. No matter how warm or welcoming a room appears to be, if nobody uses it, it ends up being wasted space, like your little-used dining room.

"I'm always amazed how many people think the answer to their design problems is to either add on or move out instead of taking a hard look at existing unused or under-used space. In your case, should the need arise to turn the den back into a dining room, it can be done without too much time or trouble." Finished with my little design spiel, I stepped further into the room.

The walls were painted a chocolate brown that made the white crown molding, baseboard, door, and window trim pop. A bronze-finished fan with blades of woven rattan hung from the ceiling. A club chair, along with a pair of love seats, provided ample seating. The chair was covered in black, red, and green plaid velvet. The love seats were done in a caramel-colored leather. A round, red tufted leather cocktail table was strategically placed in front of the twin love seats. The low table matched in style and color the leather chaise lounge that filled one corner of the room. Behind the chaise stood a mission-style floor lamp.

A leather-topped, mahogany drum table positioned next to the club chair held a brass-and-glass lamp. The lamp with its parchment shade provided additional lighting as did the pair of bronze-finished wall sconces that flanked the black-granite-topped mahogany lowboy. The floor lamp, along with the table lamp and wall sconces, bathed the room in a triangle of light. The mahogany cabinet housed a collection of books, magazines, DVDs, a DVD player, and a television set. The black granite top played host to a few well-chosen brass bells and crystal figurines, souvenirs from Amanda's European vacation trips.

A woven wool rug with its intricate pattern executed in black with shades of red, green, and creamy beige anchored the room and complemented the rich, dark oak flooring. For me, the frosting on the cake (or in this case, the den) was the room's double window that faced the front of the house. The opening had been beautifully dressed in a honey-colored bamboo shade with lined, floor-to-ceiling side panels of sage-colored linen.

"Kudos to you, kiddo," I said, giving Amanda a high five. "I could not have done it better myself."

"Then you're not upset that I didn't hire Designer Jeans to do the transformation? I was going to ask for your help but then this flipping thing came along and I immediately thought of Designer Jeans for the design and staging part of the Semple project." Amanda paused and brushed back a strand of golden blond hair that had escaped her single braid 'do. I could see that she was struggling to keep her emotions in check.

"I thought you and JR would enjoy the experience," she said when she was able to continue, "along with making a nice profit. But although I didn't ask for your help before, I'm asking for it now."

"What kind of help?" Even to me, it sounded like a dumb question but like my mother, Annie Kelly, often said—the only thing worse than a dumb question is a dumb answer. I mentally crossed my fingers and hoped that Amanda Little's answer didn't fall into that category.

"Help me convince the police and most of the people in this town that while I may have been stupid about Stuart, I was never in cahoots with him and I certainly didn't kill the man," she said vehemently, providing me with an opening just as I'd hoped.

If I was going to stick my nose in my son-in-law's business, I wanted some answers from Amanda Little, including an explanation of what she had to take care of on that fateful Saturday that prevented her from meeting JR and me at the Semple place before six that evening. I also needed to know about her relationship with the murder victim. From the remarks she'd made when we entered the house for her preview of the staging job, it seemed obvious to me that the two had had a falling out. But was it a murderous one? I was about to find out.

"Why don't we start with you filling me in on a few things, beginning with your relationship with Stuart Goodenough," I said settling down in the comfortable club chair.

"Okay," said Amanda, taking a deep breath. "Stu and I seemed to hit it off right from the start. Unlike men I've dated in the past, he knew how to treat a woman. He brought me flowers and candy. He also took me to the best restaurants in Indianapolis. If I wanted to see a play or go to a concert, he got and paid for the best seats in the house. He was as free with his money as he was with his compliments. Just being with him made me feel terrific."

Getting up from the love seat, Amanda began to pace up and down the gorgeous area rug, careful not to step beyond its perimeter. I could tell from her body language, she was uncomfortable talking about her private life. I wanted to give her a hug and tell her everything was going to be fine, but like the police, I had a job to do. With a sappy, understanding look plastered on my face, I waited for Amanda to continue which she did.

"The last date I had with Stuart was set for this past Wednesday night. As usual, he acted as though spending time with me was the most precious thing in his life. He said we'd be having dinner at his place in Castle Hills and that there was something important he wanted to ask me." Amanda paused and, taking a fresh tissue from the pocket of her white-and-gold pantsuit, she dabbed at her eyes, careful not to smear her perfectly applied makeup.

"Of course, I thought I knew what that question was going to be. And I also knew what my answer would be and, believe it or not, it was going to be no. Oh, I loved the thought of Stuart being madly in love with me and begging me to marry him but the truth was that I wasn't 'in love' with the guy. So anyway," said Amanda who had traded pacing the floor for a seat on the chaise longue, "to make a long story short, I arrived at his place at eight p.m. on the button. When Marty, the doorman, offered to buzz Stuart to let him know that I'd arrived, I told him not to bother and took the elevator to Stu's penthouse apartment.

"I was about to knock on the door when I heard Stuart's voice. He was talking very loud to someone on the phone. He told the person, and these were his exact words, 'I'm going to put the bite on the real estate broad tonight. I already told her that I had something big to ask her. Little does she know that the 'm' word is money, not marriage. I'm going to use the old chestnut of a bank transfer snafu tying up my account. She's so nuts about me, I'm thinking of jacking up the amount I need to cover the shortfall in the flip project funds. After all, I did spend some of that dough on her.' Once again Amanda stopped and dabbed at her eyes with the tissue.

"Overhearing that phone conversation was the very first time that I was aware Stuart had money problems, honest. He also said something to the person about playing it smart and forget about the danger or words to that effect. To tell you the truth, I wasn't really listening at that point. All I wanted to do was get out of there. I had every intention of going straight home and having a good cry when who should I meet in the lobby but Arthur Kraft. If Marty the doorman hadn't stopped him, we would have literally bumped into each other."

Normally, I would not have interrupted but I was so flabbergasted, I couldn't stop myself. "Arthur Kraft? You want to run that by me again?"

To say that I was amazed would be an understatement. Of all the people in all the world, she just happens to bump into Arthur Kraft in the lobby of the same building where Stu Goodenough just happens to be living in the penthouse. You couldn't make this stuff up, I said to myself. I also asked for and received a cup of hot coffee, permission to smoke, and an ashtray. I was in for the long haul.

Once my caffeine addiction was satisfied, I asked Amanda if she knew why Arthur Kraft was at that particular location on that particular night. While her answer was vague, my gut instinct told me that she was being honest.

"Gosh, I was so upset, I really don't remember what he said. Then, while I was following Arthur back to Seville, I used my car phone and called Stuart. I said I had a migraine and would see him the next day. Instead of having dinner with Stuart, Arthur and I had dinner together at Milano's that night, which ended up being the turning point in our relationship." Amanda was blushing like a schoolgirl. "Arthur confessed that from the get-go he'd set his sights and heart on me."

"Maybe your bumping into him in the lobby of Stuart's apartment building wasn't exactly an accident, at least not on his part." In view of the fact that I believed that someone other than Amanda had killed Stuart, I had to consider that the quiet, unassuming Arthur Kraft might very well be that someone. Even if the soft-spoken florist was as innocent as a newborn babe, he certainly had some explaining to do. I made a mental note to add Arthur Kraft's name to the growing list of people I intended to interview.

Sensing that Amanda had gone on the defensive regarding the subject of Arthur Kraft, I moved on to my next question. Sounding more like Perry Mason than an interior designer and grandmother of three, I asked Amanda, "When and where was the last time that you spoke with the deceased, Stuart Goodenough?"

"That would have been the next day, Thursday, before I called you about the staging and with the news that Stuart had set the open house for Sunday. I still had the lab-made sapphire and zircon cocktail ring he'd given me two weeks ago on my birthday. For a relatively affordable piece of jewelry, the ring was large in size. A real eye-catcher. It reminded me of the kind of thing that Bambi Eastwood would wear. When Stuart slipped the ring on my finger, he said that if he could, he would give me the moon," Amanda added with a laugh that was as chilling as it was brief. "In view of what I'd overheard on Wednesday night, I wanted to see his face when I gave him back the ring along with a piece of my mind."

"And did you?" I inquired, helping myself to a second cup of coffee from the carafe that Amanda had placed within easy reach and lighting a cigarette. With Amanda being a nonsmoker, I got up from the plaid chair and cracked open the double window. When someone is nice enough to allow me to smoke, I always make an effort to keep the level of the proven pollutant in the air down to a minimum.

"No. What happened was the next morning, bright and early, I found Stuart where I expected him to be—at the flip project site. He and Duke Demarco were in the middle of a horrific argument about money. Duke was waving what looked like a fistful of invoices in Stuart's face. He accused Stuart of stealing project funds and trying to stiff him on the bills. Stuart in turn accused Duke of padding expenses. When Duke noticed me standing in the foyer, he stormed out of the house. By then I'd heard enough. Realizing that I was dealing with a smooth-talking con man, I decided to switch tactics. Instead of getting mad, I would get even."

I could see from the satisfied look on her face and the defiance in her voice that Amanda Little was clearly enjoying this part of what so far had been a sad tale of betrayal.

"I began by apologizing to Stu for standing him up the night before," said Amanda with obvious relish. "Then I handed him the ring, saying that I had to be honest with him. When he asked about what, I hit him with the story that the entire time he was wining and dining me, I'd been two-timing him with a gorgeous-looking guy who was as fabulously wealthy as I was and who could well afford real diamonds and real sapphires. I also told him that my beau was a good ten years younger than me and had great political connections, which was why we were planning to be married in the White House Rose Garden next spring."

"And what was Stuart's reaction. Was he surprised or angry or what? Before you answer, I want you to realize that the only reason I'm asking you all these questions is because you asked for my help and not because I'm a nosy Parker."

Amanda nodded her head and gave me a lackluster smile. "I don't know if I can explain it to you any better than I did to the police when they asked me the same questions but I'll give it a try." Scrunching up her beautiful face, she seemed to be searching for the right words. "I guess the best way to put it is that to me, Stuart looked like a kid who'd just been told that there's no Santa Claus. He picked up the ring and stared at it for what seemed like forever. Then he put it in the pocket of his sport coat, announced that the open house was set for Sunday, and walked out the door. When I ran out to the front porch, I asked him where he was going; he mumbled something about playing some lucrative golf and drove off in his car. That was the last time I saw him alive."

"Did you tell all of this to the police, including the part about Duke Demarco?"

"Of course, but Chief Stevens seemed more interested in my confrontation with Stuart than Duke's," replied Amanda, tearing the tissue she was holding into tiny pieces. "In fact, he seemed to dismiss what I said like maybe I'd either exaggerated or made up the whole thing. Sergeant Rosen was listening and he didn't seem to act as though he believed me, either."

The part about Sid Rosen, Matt's sidekick, being on the scene was news to me. He must have arrived when JR and I were ordered to remain in the living room area. The solidly built, quiet spoken, Vietnam vet was the kind of cop who kept his mouth shut and eyes open. Even if he believed that every word out of Amanda's mouth was true, he would not have let it show.

I could see that Amanda was getting frustrated. "Amanda, dear," I said in a soothing voice, "if I'm going to sort out this whole murder mess, I need to know what was so important on Saturday that it prevented you from meeting JR and me at the Semple house any earlier than six p.m. If I remember right, you mentioned that there was something you had to take care of or it could come back to haunt you." The golden blond's answer almost blew me away.

"I had an appointment at Lady Lovely Locks in Indianapolis to have my brown roots touched up along with the gold highlights. I also had my nails done. I wanted to look good for Sunday's open house," Amanda replied, staring at me as though she'd just noticed my own less-than-cover-girl appearance. "My mother always said that one should look their very best regardless of the situation."

I tried to think of some words of wisdom from my own mother on the same subject but came up empty. I sat there looking like a damp load of laundry and waited for the impeccably groomed real estate agent to continue.

"You can check on that if you feel it's necessary," she said. "My hairdresser's name is Althea. I had a two o'clock appointment and didn't get out of there 'til almost five. When I got back into town, it was so close to six that I went directly over to the old Victorian and waited in my car for you and JR."

"Was that when you first discovered the gold key chain with the house key on it was missing? Think hard," I said in a tone of voice that I hoped conveyed the importance of the question. It did.

"Yes, I'm positive. I damn near fainted when I looked in the window seat, moved that purple pillow, and found myself staring at not only the obviously deceased Stuart Goodenough but my missing chain and key as well. Who could have put my key and chain in there and why?" asked Amanda.

"Someone who somehow ended up with your key and chain. More than likely that someone was the murderer. The key and chain were probably planted in the window seat in an effort to throw the police off his or her trail and onto yours. So far, it seems to be working."

I didn't mention to Amanda that two names, Arthur Kraft and Duke Demarco, had popped to the top of my list of suspects like a couple of bad eggs in a bowl of water. At the time, they were also the only names on the list.

Satisfied that Amanda had given me the information I needed to support my fledgling investigation into Stuart Goodenough's murder, I stood under the dripping canopy and bid the real estate agent good-bye, but not before promising to stay in touch.

"You've got my cell number and I've got yours. If you think of anything, regardless of its importance, give me a call," I advised the forlorn-looking Amanda. "Or if you feel like having a girls' night out, give a holler and JR, Mary England, and I will be ready and willing to accompany you anywhere, anytime. Within reason, of course," I said with a wink and a grin in an attempt to lighten up the situation.

"Of course. And, Jean, thanks so much for coming over here this morning. I can't tell you how much better your visit and faith in me has made me feel. Between your investigation and dear Arthur's moral support, I'm starting to believe that I might actually get through this terrible ordeal and prove my innocence. Speak of the devil," exclaimed Amanda, breaking into a megawatt smile, "here he comes now, bumbershoot and all."

Leaving the lovely Amanda and the apparently love-struck Arthur Kraft standing alone together on the rain-splattered stoop where they were making what can best be described as goo-goo eyes at one another, I headed to my van and lunch at JR's. I was in need of food for my brain as well as my body. Other than an occasional infusion of Irish intuition, caffeine, and nicotine, my little gray cells were running on empty.

Perhaps, I reasoned as I made the short drive, the stop at JR's would give me that proverbial shot in the arm or at the very least, a grilled cheese sandwich made with extra cheese and homemade bread. The supersize sandwich was a regular item on the Cusak luncheon menu. Either way, I couldn't lose.

Chapter sixteen

"Good grief, Mom, what happened to you? You look like a drowned rat," commented JR when she came to the front door and welcomed me into the house. "Where's your umbrella?" As did Amanda Little, my daughter peered around as if the missing item was lurking somewhere in the immediate vicinity.

"Take a guess," I challenged, "and if you're right, I'll reward you with my company for lunch. I'll also forgive you for the drowned rat comment.

"Lost another brolly, did you now," she said, referring to the missing rain gear and sounding so much like my mother, who really did come from Ireland, that it gave me goose bumps. Reaching into the mound of clean laundry that was in danger of spilling out of the plastic basket and onto the not-so-clean kitchen floor, JR found a hand towel and suggested I use it to dry my mass of wet, frizzy hair.

"If you want lunch, you're going to have to work for it, starting with folding that load of towels. When you're done you can put them away in the upstairs linen closet."

It took me almost as long to dry my tresses as it did to take care of the basket of laundry. When I was finished with both chores, JR fixed me a crisp side salad and a delicious, crunchy, grilled cheese sandwich.

Waiting until I'd cleaned my plate of everything but the pattern, JR set out a platter of freshly baked, homemade lemon squares and poured us both a steaming cup of herbal tea. With Matt back to work, Kerry and Kelly in school, and Kris tucked in his crib, where he was sleeping off the effects of an infant power lunch (mashed peas and mushy strained carrots), except for the dog, the cat, and an assortment of little critters in little cages, we basically had the house to ourselves.

Before telling JR everything I'd gleaned from my morning visit with Amanda Little, I asked my daughter how Matt was doing and was told that he was in the process of catching up on the homicide investigation into Stuart's death. It came as no surprise to me that Rollie Stevens had turned the investigation over to Matt. With Matt back at the helm, the police chief immediately left for the Upper Peninsula of Michigan where he was one of the guest speakers at a seminar on behalf of the wolverine, a dangerous, ill-tempered carnivore. You name the animal and the chief is there to protect it from harm.

"Matt got a call this morning from the medical examiner's office on his cell phone. He was in the shower at the time, so like the good wife that I am, I answered it," said JR. The gold flecks in her blue green eyes seemed to be dancing with excitement.

"Jeez, don't tell me that you actually talked to Dr. Loo. What did she have to say? Was she finished with the autopsy? What were her findings? Tell me everything she said."

"Mother, if you don't cool it and let me talk, I'm going to turn you out in the rain and let you hitch a ride home in the next passing rowboat."

The persistent showers had turned into one long and nasty thunderstorm. Even though I had my doubts about

JR's remark about turning me out, I wasn't taking any chances. "Sorry. It's just that I'm so anxious to hear what Loo had to say. Please go on."

"It wasn't Loo herself on the phone. It was one of her lackeys. At first he was reluctant to talk to me but after I turned on the Hastings charm, I had the guy singing like the Mormon choir. He told me that the victim bought the farm on Saturday sometime after lunch but before dinner. The cause of death was suffocation and the murder weapon was the ugly accent pillow found with the body. There were no marks on the body such as defensive wounds, and the dark and purplish mottling suggested that the body was already in the window seat at the time of death." JR sat back in her chair and took a sip of the body- and soul-warming tea. From the look on her face, I could tell that she was extremely pleased with herself.

The news that the body was in the window seat before death reinforced my belief that someone the size of the petite Amanda Little could not have possibly overpowered Stuart Goodenough, forced him into the window seat, and then smothered him with a pillow.

"What did Matt have to say when you told him about the call? You did tell him what the guy from Loo's office had to say, right?"

"Wrong," she said with a sly smile. "I didn't have to. When I heard Matt step out of the shower, I pretended that I was mentally overwhelmed by the information and that Matt was now available to take the message himself. Then I opened the bathroom door, handed Matt the phone, and like the good and quick-thinking wife that I am, beat it down to the kitchen and made Matt one hell of a great breakfast. Trust me, he didn't have murder on his mind when he kissed me good-bye. So what do you think, Mom? Did your little girl do good or what?"

For the second time that day, I delivered a high five to a deserving female. I also threw in a hug as a bonus and silently thanked St. Patrick for the unexpected delivery of luck. With my little gray cells replenished and my body fortified by a tasty, tummy-filling lunch, I was ready to get back to my own method of sleuthing, something Mary once described as a whole lot of talking to people and very little action. I prefer to think of it as using logic to solve a difficult puzzle.

I proceeded to fill JR in on my morning tête-à-tête with Amanda Little, a person of interest as the politically correct would say. My daughter agreed with me that I needed to have a serious talk with Arthur Kraft.

"I think Dr. Loo's findings pretty well reinforces my belief in Amanda Little's innocence," I said, helping myself to another lemon square to go with the fresh cup of tea JR set before me despite my protest that I couldn't eat or drink another thing.

"How so? I didn't pick up anything from my conversation with the guy from Loo's office that excluded or cleared her. She might have tricked him into climbing into the window seat. Although Matt's been pretty mum on the subject, I'm afraid Amanda continues to be the number one suspect, thanks in a large part to her key chain turning up in the window seat and her admission to Rollie Stevens that she had a serious confrontation with Stuart the Thursday before the murder."

"She wasn't the only one," I reminded JR. "Duke Demarco also had a dustup with Stuart Goodenough that same morning."

"As Matt would say, prove it. So far, Mom, you've only got Amanda's word that she witnessed Stuart and Duke having a terrible argument. Maybe she made the whole thing up." JR paused and checked the baby monitor on the counter. Satisfied for the moment that Kris was sleeping soundly, she came back to the table and the subject of Amanda Little's guilt or innocence.

"You're starting to sound like Rollie Stevens," I said, even though I was aware that she was playing the devil's advocate and had delivered the proverbial shot in the arm that I needed.

"Don't get me wrong, Mom. Like you, I believe Aman-

da's telling the truth but believing doesn't make it so.
You've got to prove it."

JR may have inherited her charm from Charlie, but she
obviously inherited her logical mind from yours truly.
"And that is exactly what I'm trying to do," I said, gathering up the empty platter, luncheon plates, teapot, and cups
and depositing them next to the monitor on the counter.
The sound of happy baby babble floated through the air,
signaling the end of Kris's nap and the end of my visit.

"Well, it's back to the salt mines for me," I said, giving
JR a good-bye hug and stepping out onto the sturdy, large,
well-protected front porch—a welcoming shelter and
something that continues to be appreciated by owner and
visitor alike.

Once I was back in my van, I lit a cigarette and reconsidered the salt mine remark I'd made to JR. She'd given
me food for thought along with good information and
sound advice. I had a lot of thinking to do, beginning with
Amanda Little's version of the events leading up to the
murder and ending with what JR had said about believing
not being enough. I also considered the possibility that I
was in over my head. I then came to the conclusion that
Dorothy was right when she told Auntie Em that there's no
place like home. With that in mind, I put my investigation
on temporary hold and headed for Blueberry Lane and
Kettle Cottage.

Chapter seventeen

꙳

If I thought that my going home was going to let me escape from my investigation into the murder of Stu Goodenough, I was mistaken. I'd parked the van on the side drive and was making my way toward the back door of the house when I realized that the kitchen phone was ringing. Fumbling with both the top and bottom latches of the Dutch door, I ran through the kitchen in an effort to catch the call before it went into voice mail. I figured Charlie was hard at work in the cellar and had deliberately decided not to answer the telephone. Racing through the kitchen, I tripped over the lounging Pesty and fell into the waiting arms of the Mickey Mouse phone.

"Oh, Gin, I'm so glad I caught you," Mary said in her familiar, dithery manner after I finally managed to steady myself enough to croak a "hello" into the phone.

I was tempted to correct Mary and credit Mickey with the save but I didn't. It wasn't worth the explanation.

"I must have called the house at least a half a dozen times since this morning. By the way, I didn't bother leaving messages since it was obvious to me that you weren't home so if you check your voice mail and there isn't any, that was only me. You understand what I'm saying?"

"I understand completely, Mar," I replied. The scary part was that I actually did. "But I am rather surprised you didn't catch Charlie at least one of the times that you phoned. He's spending the day cleaning out the cellar."

"Maybe that's what he started out to do, Gin, but right now he's down at the store with Denny."

"Oh no," I moaned, "don't tell me, let me guess. Denny got that shipment of those large, flat-screen television sets and Charlie's at the store picking out the one he wants for our den. Maybe I'd better get down there before he buys one so big that we'll have to watch it from the front lawn."

"Yes, we did get that shipment in but that has nothing to do with why Charlie's at England's Fine Furniture and not in the cellar or for that matter why I've been trying to get in touch with you all day. I would've called you on your cell but I couldn't find my cell and . . ."

"And you weren't sure if you could contact me on my cell using a regular phone," I said, finishing Mary's sentence. I probably should have explained the compatibility between telephone systems but I was anxious to find out why Mary was calling and what had prompted Charlie to quit the cellar for the furniture store.

"Right," said Mary. "Anyway, the reason I've been trying to get a hold of you is that I did a bit of sleuthing on my own when I was grocery shopping this morning and I couldn't wait to tell you what I learned."

Knowing that it wouldn't do any good to remind Mary that playing Dr. Watson to my Sherlock Holmes when we're together is far different (and a lot safer) than sleuthing on her own, I saved the lecture for a later time and asked Mary what it was that she'd uncovered while perusing the fresh fruits and vegetables aisle.

"The grocery store was rather crowded in spite of the bad weather or maybe because of it," said Mary before getting to the heart of the matter.

As usual, this would take some time. Eventually, I

learned that Mary had overheard a conversation between Ima Kind, Ben's wife, and Susan Demarco, Duke's wife. The two women had been standing near the deli counter where Mary was waiting for the clerk to finish slicing some lunch meat that she'd ordered.

"I didn't mean to eavesdrop but when I accidentally overheard them mention Stuart Goodenough's murder, my ears perked up. They were worried that their husbands might be suspects since both men had had a run-in with Stuart and neither one of them had an alibi for Saturday. I was so busy listening to them that I forgot to tell the deli clerk to stop slicing when the scale registered a quarter of a pound. By the time Ima and Susan moved out of hearing range, I ended up with nearly three pounds of thin-sliced bologna. Thank goodness it's Denny favorite sandwich meat."

Thanking Mary for the information and exacting a promise that she wouldn't do anymore sleuthing unless she was with me, I managed to move the conversation from the murder investigation to what had prompted Charlie to abandon the cellar for England's Fine Furniture.

According to Mary, it had to do with an 8-by-10 photograph that Charlie came across while cleaning out the cellar. Apparently, the photo was part of a large collection of memorabilia-filled albums from the Kennedy era and appeared to be in mint condition.

When Mary mentioned the albums, I immediately knew what she was talking about or rather I thought I did. A few years after my father had passed away, my mother presented me with the albums. She claimed that the contents were worth their weight in gold. Maybe so, but I've always suspected that my mother's generosity was motivated by the high cost of shipping the oversized, overstuffed albums to the condo she'd purchased in sunny California.

Not knowing what else to do with the unexpected "windfall," I'd lugged the heavy albums down to the cellar where I unceremoniously deposited them, contents and all, in an empty steamer trunk. There they remained, virtually forgotten, until the industrious Charlie discovered them.

"My stars, Gin, the way Charlie came into the store like a man on fire and waving that photo in the air as if it were the Holy Grail, he scared the living daylights out of Herbie. I'm afraid that being abducted in the middle of the night by aliens has put a strain on poor Herbie's nervous system."

"Yeah, whatever. Everything has its price," I remarked, not bothering to hide my growing impatience, "including sleepovers with little green men. Now can we talk about Charlie and the photograph?"

"Of course," Mary replied, deliberately ignoring my sarcastic remark directed at Herbie and his nocturnal adventures. "Knowing that Denny is somewhat of an expert on the Kennedy presidency, Charlie brought the photograph to the store to show him the note and signature on it. He wanted Denny's opinion of its worth."

"Oh my lord," I shrieked into the phone, startling the drowsy Pesty, "Charlie found a signed photo of JFK!" My mind flashed back to what my mother said about the contents of the albums being worth their weight in gold. At the time, I thought she was handing me a load of malarkey along with the albums. "Mar, do you realize if the photo is the real deal, it could fetch megabucks?"

"That's what Denny thinks, too, Gin. He advised Charlie to have the photo professionally appraised like they do on the *Antiques Roadshow.* It's amazing what treasures can be found in an attic or a cellar.

"Okay. But now maybe you could begin with why Charlie showed the picture to Denny in the first place," I said, trying to hide my impatience.

"Why, I'd be more than happy to," burbled Mary. "Charlie sought out Denny because of what was written on the back of the picture." Mary seemed satisfied that she had explained everything.

It wasn't easy but I managed to keep my cool. "And then what happened after Charlie showed Denny the photo?" I asked ever so politely, which isn't all that easy to do when biting one's tongue.

"Denny went through his collection of books on the Kennedy era," Mary said, blissfully unaware how thin my patience had been stretched, "and found where the itinerary of JFK's trip to County Wexford in Ireland matches with your parents' itinerary. Someway, somehow your folks managed to get President Kennedy to write a personal note, complete with signature and date, on the front of the picture. The fact that he mentions Mrs. Kennedy in it makes the note unique. It also increases its value, especially to serious collectors of Kennedy memorabilia; at least that's Denny's opinion, but like I said, he told Charlie to have a professional appraiser take a look at it."

"Wow! So that's why Charlie's not home. He's probably in Indianapolis doing that right now," I said, thinking aloud.

"No, I don't think so. When I was leaving the store, I thought Charlie said something about maybe watching the football game with Denny and Herbie on one of the new flat TVs that came in, but don't quote me. If you want company tonight, give me a call and I'll come over. I'll even bring dinner, that is if you don't mind having bologna sandwiches."

Fortunately, Mary was wrong about my husband spending the evening with Denny, Herbie Waddlemeyer, and a humongous flat-screen television. Within minutes of my getting off the phone with his twin sister, Charlie came rushing through the back door of Kettle Cottage with a bottle of Webber's Bay Chardonnay, a couple of thick-cut porterhouse steaks, and the much talked-about "Kennedy" photo as it became known within our family circle.

Depositing the wine and steaks on the counter and out of Pesty's line of sight, Charlie carefully removed the photograph from its folder and proudly presented it to me. I immediately recognized the photo, the note, and the signature.

"Oh, for heaven's sake, now I remember this old photograph. I can't believe that I actually smiled with my mouth full of braces or that I was ever that dopey-looking," I said,

examining the old studio photo portrait. "This is the picture that my folks brought with them when they went to
Ireland. I think they showed it to every friend and family
member in County Wexford. A cousin on the Kelly side of
the family, James Francis, thought I was the spitting image
of his own daughter, Jackie, so much so that he scribbled a
note about it right on the front of the photo. See, he even
signed it with his initials—JFK. Uh-oh! Sorry, Charlie, I
think I just rained on your parade."

But by then, Charlie had already left the room and was
in the process of lighting the promised fire. Had I not been
holding the 8-by-10 photo, I felt certain it would have gone
up in smoke along with the fireplace logs and Charlie's
dream of untold riches. By the time we'd eaten the steaks,
drank the wine, and settled down to watch the *Antiques
Roadshow*, my husband was back to being his old self—
charming but wiser.

Chapter eighteen

~✺

Tuesday was as sunny and dry as Monday had been overcast and rainy. The previous day's inclement weather did almost nothing to relieve the near-drought conditions that had been plaguing the Midwest since the beginning of summer. Applying the old adage of out of sight, out of mind to both the rain and the cellar, Charlie had decided to spend the day with Denny on Sleepy Hollow's golf course. I, in turn, applied the same adage to my husband and housework (including the laundry) and had decided to spend the day investigating the murder of Stuart Goodenough.

I'd almost finished making notes on what I'd learned so far about the murder when I received the phone call from JR.

"GHB? I've never heard of it," I admitted to my daughter when she hit me with the news that the medical examiner, Dr. Sue Lin Loo, had found the drug gamma hydroxybutyric acid, or GHB, in the murder victim's system.

"Why am I not surprised," JR replied with a giggle. "Most people in your age group aren't even aware of date-rape drugs. Your generation knows more about the dangers of consuming too much sodium than the dangers of consuming a drink laced with GHB."

Because she was right, I didn't bother defending the aging baby-boomer generation. Instead, I wisely decided to listen and learn.

"Date-rape drugs have been part of the dance club and bar scene in major cities since the late 1990s," JR informed me, "and in the past couple of years they've made their way into smaller cities and towns. Matt says what makes GHB so dangerous is regardless of its form, be it liquid, powder, or pill, the drug is colorless and odorless. You can't taste it, either, so when it's added to a drink, it's virtually undetectable to the victim.

"This particular date-rape drug is actually legal in the U.S. and approved for use as an anesthetic to dull pain during surgery or to treat narcolepsy. It can cause a host of problems such as dizziness, loss of memory or loss of consciousness, coma, and even death. Put this stuff in an alcoholic drink and the side effects really pack a punch. Matt thinks it was used to knock Stuart out, something that allowed the murderer to push him into the window seat where he was suffocated with the pillow. The presence of GHB also helps explains the absence of defensive wounds on the body. Pretty scary stuff."

"It certainly is. How in the world did you manage to get all this info out of Matt? He's not exactly known for sharing information with anyone other than the boys in blue and certainly not with Designer Jeans."

"I used one of the oldest tricks in the book—pillow talk. Need I say more?"

"No, I think I've heard more than enough," I replied crumpling up the notes I'd made on why I believed that it was physically impossible for Amanda Little to have committed the murder. After listening to what JR had to say about GHB and its availability, I knew that like it or not, I would have to add the beautiful real estate agent's name to my list of suspects. I also needed JR's help.

"I realize that you're pretty well housebound with Kris

and all, but do you think you could do some sleuthing via the telephone for me? It would really be a big help."

"Mother, I've been waiting for you to ask. Name it and I'll do it but like I always say, let's not tell Matt. What he doesn't know can't hurt me."

I knew that JR's remark was meant to be a lighthearted one, but that didn't stop the chill that ran down my spine or my silent prayer to St. Agnes, the patron saint of young women, to keep an eye on my daughter.

"Earth to Mother," said JR, breaking the pause in our conversation. "I know you're not going to tell Matt what I'm doing to help your investigation, but it would nice if you told me. Mom?"

"Oh sorry, JR. I was pouring myself a cup of coffee and lighting a cigarette," I said, covering my moment of prayer with a little white lie. "I need you to call the beauty salon that Amanda Little goes to in Indianapolis and verify her alibi for Saturday afternoon. The name of the place is Lady Lovely Locks. I don't have the phone number but I do have the name of the beautician. Her name is Althea and Amanda is a regular customer of hers."

"Okay, got it. What's Althea's last name? It would be nice to have it in case there's more than one Althea."

"That I don't know, but if there's more than one, I'd be surprised. If the name were Ashley, Brittany, or Tiffany, it probably would be a different story. Anyway, Amanda claims that she was at the salon with Althea from two in the afternoon until almost five."

Before ending the call, JR asked what I would be doing and I told her that I'd planned to drop in on Arthur Kraft at his flower shop.

"Do me a favor, Mom, and take Aunt Mary with you," said JR. I could hear the concern in her voice. When I objected, she did everything she could to convince me not to go it alone, pointing out that Matt always took Sid Rosen along when he had to interview "a person of interest." She even reminded me that there is some truth in the old saying about safety in numbers.

"Okay, okay, I'll take Mary with me," I said as I cancelled out my earlier fib by actually pouring myself a cup of coffee and lighting a cigarette.

"You better, Mom, or I'll tell Pops what you've been up to lately, which hasn't anything to do with interior design."

"I beg to differ with you, missy. If Designer Jeans hadn't gotten mixed up with the flip project, which has a lot to do with interior design, especially the magnificent job I did on staging the place, you wouldn't have found the body in the window seat and I wouldn't be investigating who put it in there."

"You're right about that," conceded JR, "but I still want you to promise me that you'll take Aunt Mary with you and I promise to check out Amanda Little's alibi." Not waiting for my response, JR announced that she would stay in touch and with that said, she ended the call.

Once off the phone, I headed upstairs to the master bathroom for a long, hot shower. I used the time in the shower to weigh the pros and cons of taking Mary along with me to the flower shop where I hoped to interview Arthur Kraft. Even though I had only a nodding acquaintance with the florist, on the surface he certainly didn't seem to be the Dr. Jekyll/Mr. Hyde type. Prior to the murder, I would have classified him as being more of a milquetoast than a maniac, but now I wasn't so sure. I intended to ask him some tough questions and decided that he probably would be more inclined to answer them if I showed up at the flower shop all by my lonesome.

By the time I'd finished my shower, found something to wear (my old, reliable, green chenille jumpsuit), and applied only enough makeup to feel comfortable being seen in the harsh light of day, I'd made up my mind not to call Mary. Technically, I hadn't actually promised JR that I would do so. To say that I was surprised to find my best friend and sister-in-law sitting at the round, oak kitchen table when I came down the stairs would be a colossal understatement to say the least.

"My stars, you sure take a long time to get dressed. I've been waiting for you with the doughnuts and coffee that JR said you wanted me to pick up at the Koffee Kabin. She didn't specify what kind of doughnuts or coffee so I got us each a double mocha latte and a couple of plain doughnuts. I hope you don't mind taking a pass on frosting but I'm watching my weight."

I was tempted to remind Mary that she's been watching her weight for years and it hasn't changed. She is as short, round, and fey as her husband Denny is tall, lean, and realistic. They are, in my opinion, the perfect Jack Sprat couple.

"Oh, and I didn't forget Pesty," said Mary, removing two containers of coffee and two tissue-wrapped doughnuts from the carryout box with the popular coffeehouse's logo. "Since she's also on a diet, I'll share my doughnut with her but not the coffee. I don't think the caffeine would be very good for her, wouldn't you agree?"

"Of course," I replied, "and any veterinarian worth his or her salt would agree as well, particularly in Pesty's case because of the danger involved."

"Oh? And what exactly is that danger?" asked Mary. "Other than being a little bit overweight, a common problem for some of us, that dog looks perfectly healthy to me."

"Because the caffeine could rob her of the ability to nap between meals and snacks. A sleep-deprived Pesty might actually collapse from hunger while waiting for some pushover to show up with a calorie-laden treat such as an unfrosted doughnut."

It took her less than a nanosecond to catch on to the fact that I was being facetious. The pleasingly plump Mary took revenge by sharing her doughnut, along with half of mine, with the slavering pooch. She also presented me with my half of the bill—a whopping eight dollars.

Twenty minutes later, thanks to my daughter's intervention, Mary was in the van's passenger seat as I headed for downtown Seville and my interview with the unsuspecting

Arthur Kraft. Although I wasn't exactly afraid of going one-on-one with the soft-spoken bachelor, he was on my list of murder suspects. With that in mind, I came to the conclusion that having Mary tag along was actually a good idea, even if it wasn't mine.

Chapter nineteen

The flower shop operated by Arthur Kraft had been in the Kraft family almost from the time that Garrison Seville, a Civil War hero, founded our town in the 1870s. Over the years, the once prosperous and prominent family experienced a reduction in size and fortune due in part to death, divorce, and taxes. While Arthur lived a quiet life alone in the family home, a Queen Anne–style house built during Seville's original building boom, the gossip making the rounds in town regarding the flower shop was anything but quiet. The word on the street was that Arthur, who owned the shop lock, stock, building, and land, was going to sell his downtown holdings to an out-of-state corporation. If true, such a sale had the potential to restore the Kraft fortune along with the potential to destroy Seville's thriving downtown shopping district. Unlike many of the small towns and cities across the Hoosier state, Seville has managed to just say no to the big box stores, enclosed malls with stores that cater to the fifteen-to-twenty-five age group, and tacky strip malls that pop up overnight with businesses that disappear in the night. Arthur Kraft had denied the rumors that his business was up for sale but to no avail. Like my mother would say, a runaway train does less damage than a runaway tongue and is easier to stop.

From the moment that Mary and I entered the flower shop I wondered how anyone would believe, even for a minute, that Arthur Kraft was thinking of getting out of the florist business. The place was overflowing with fresh plants, floral arrangements, and containers of blooming flowers. A tinkling bell over the door announced our arrival to the shop's owner, who was in the middle of taking a phone order for a kiddy birthday bash that was set to take place the following day.

While Arthur discussed the shape and color of the three dozen helium-filled balloons that were part of the order, Mary and I browsed around the shop, admiring the selection of vases, planters, and knickknacks displayed on the glass shelves that lined the walls. Mary was debating whether or not to purchase a ceramic golf cart planter with tendrils of English ivy cascading down its sides when the florist came bustling up beside us.

"Sorry for the delay but you wouldn't believe how extravagant some of these mothers can be when it involves their children's birthday parties. They pull out all the stops. Most kids, especially the little ones, would be satisfied with a homemade cake, candles, and an off-key rendering of 'Happy Birthday.' It's a shame that their mothers often turn what should be a family occasion into an event that rivals anything that Hollywood can dream up," said the flower shop proprietor in a voice so soft that I almost wished I could read lips, "but that's neither here nor there. Now what can I help you lovely ladies with today. The little golf cart, perhaps?"

This was not going as I'd hoped. I was beginning to wish that Mary was anywhere but standing beside me when to my surprise, it was she who turned everything upside down and back on the investigation track with her comment followed by her question.

"Yes, but only if you promise that you'll be around to

save the plant when it turns brown," Mary commented sweetly before hitting him with a tough question that surprised me almost as much as it did Arthur Kraft. "As one downtown business owner to another, is there any truth to the rumors that you're selling out to the highest bidder?"

"Maybe you should ask Biddy McFarland. She seems to be an expert on my plans," growled the florist. While his voice remained as soft as his brown eyes and silky brown hair, the inflection in it was as hard as steel. The slender, medium-height florist was quietly but clearly agitated.

Eager to keep the avenue of conversation open, I jumped in with a question of my own. Acting on a hunch, I asked Arthur if he had been approached by Stuart to join the Fast Flippers.

"No, actually it was the other way around. I approached him to see if he would be interested in purchasing my house for his next flip project. Nobody, and I do mean nobody, except Amanda, knew that I was serious about getting rid of the old place."

"And where and when did all this take place?" I asked, eager to hear his answer. Maybe, I said to myself, the two—Stuart and Arthur—had a deadly falling out not over a certain real estate agent but rather over a business deal that had gone wrong.

"It was the day that Amanda and Stuart had that big meeting with you, that couple from Las Vegas, Ben Kind, and Duke Demarco in the main dining room of the country club. When the meeting broke up Stuart came into the bar where I'd been eating lunch," said the florist, moving over to the door where he turned the sign from OPEN to CLOSED. Seeing the startled look on Mary's face, he explained that he was getting ready to load his van and make a delivery to Twall and Sons Mortuary.

"As I was saying," he continued, "I introduced myself as a local homeowner of a painted lady and the guy looked at me like I was speaking a foreign language. That's when I started to get suspicious about Stuart Goodenough. He was supposed to be this hotshot real estate broker and I had to explain the term *painted lady* to him."

I assured Arthur that as an interior designer, I was familiar with the term that in real estate and design circles has come to mean any grand and highly stylized house built in the latter part of the nineteenth century, especially one that has been or could be refurbished. "And was Mr. Goodenough interested in purchasing your home?"

"Not in the least. In fact, he wanted to know if I was interested in becoming a member of the Fast Flippers. When I said thanks but no thanks, he gave me his card and said he could only give me a day or so to change my mind but to call him right away if I did. The card had his name, address, and phone number."

"Arthur, if he wasn't interested in purchasing your home and if you weren't interest in what he had to offer, then can you explain why you were entering the building of Mr. Goodenough's penthouse last Wednesday night, the same night that Amanda Little left the place in tears? She told me that you came to her rescue but not why you were there."

"Sure, no problem," he replied with a grin. "You see, I have a condo in that building. Unlike Mr. Goodenough, who rented his, I own mine. I purchased it three years ago. Of course I don't get to use it as much as I'd like to but it's got that old house of mine beat all to hell. Like they say—location, location, location. Castle Hills is less than ten minutes from downtown Indy, with the sports teams, the Indianapolis Symphony, and a slew of five-star restaurants. I'm sorry, Mrs. Hastings, but I really do have to get going with my delivery to Twall's so if you've got any more questions, maybe you can come back later."

"I only have a couple of questions to ask, neither one is complicated or hard to answer so I won't be keeping you much longer," I said in my best Humphrey Bogart/Sam Spade manner. If the flower shop hadn't forbid smoking like almost every other place of business in Indiana, I would have had a lit cigarette dangling from my lips and my eyes squinting from the smoke. "First, how come you're being so cooperative in answering my questions, and second, where were you on Saturday afternoon?"

"Amanda told me that you're trying to help her clear her name so I kind of expected that you'd come calling," he replied with a smile, "and I spent most of Saturday afternoon doing what I should be doing now—making deliveries. If need be, I can give you a list of customers that I made deliveries to that day, but as you can see," he said, gesturing at his messy desk, "I'm not very organized so it would take me a while to dig it up."

Once out of the shop and on the sidewalk, while Mary busily admired the little ceramic planter that Arthur insisted she take as a present from one downtown business owner to another, I started fishing through my overstuffed leather shoulder purse in search of my elusive car keys. With my focus on the search, I literally bumped into the tall and portly Ben Kind, who was on his way to an early lunch with Mrs. Kind at the Koffee Kabin.

"Oh, my dear Mrs. Hastings, I hope you're all right," purred the moneylender as he grabbed my arm with a surprisingly hard grip, thus stopping me from falling flat on my face.

"Really, Jean, you should've been looking where you were going," sniped Ima Kind, wrinkling up her long face in a disapproving grimace as if she'd smelled something bad.

With her scribbly gray hair and sharp nose, the thin, flat-chested Ima has always reminded me of Miss Meany, a character from the old comic strip *Little Annie Rooney* that appeared some years back in the Hearst chain of newspapers. For the second time that day, it was Mary who came forward with the correct comment and question.

"My stars, Ima, don't get your pantyhose in a twist. Poor Jean hasn't been quite herself since she and JR found that dead body in the window seat of the Semple house. You did hear about it, didn't you?"

"Hasn't everyone?" retorted Ima Kind, narrowing her

eyes into tiny slits. "If Rollie Stevens had had any sense, he would have arrested Amanda Little for the murder instead of going off to attend some silly conference about saving a dumb animal. Thank goodness Ben and I spent the entire Saturday afternoon entertaining Duke Demarco and his lovely wife, Susan."

It was obvious to me that Ima was aware of the fact that Mary had been near enough in the grocery store to have overheard parts of the conversation between Susan Demarco and Ima Kind, and I didn't need my Irish intuition to figure out that the alibi was as bogus as the smile on Ben Kind's face. I also came to the conclusion that interviewing the two men, Ben and Duke, would be a waste of time. Unlike my son-in-law, I didn't have access to a lie detector machine nor did I have the power to intimidate either man into taking the test or telling the truth.

More than ever, I hoped that Amanda Little's alibi would check out. While I probably couldn't prove who'd murdered Stuart Goodenough, I hoped to at least prove that it wasn't the beautiful real estate agent.

"Jeez, I'm so sorry, Ben. I should have been watching where I was going," I said, removing my arm from Ben Kind's beefy hand. "Now, if you'll excuse us, Mary and I have places to go and people to see." I threw in the last part to test the reaction of the Kinds. While Ben's smile didn't change, Ima's demeanor certainly did. It went from smug to rattled.

"Come on, Mar, we don't want to be late for our appointment." I grabbed the astonished Mary by the elbow and all but pulled her down the street to where I'd parked the van.

Plunging my hand into my purse, I managed to snag my keys. Once we were safely in the van, I admitted to Mary that I'd fibbed about having an appointment but not about having places to go and people to see.

"We really do have places to go and people to see." I said, "but first things first. Let's have lunch. How about if we go to the club for the seafood buffet?"

Expecting Mary to eagerly respond, I was surprised when she suggested that we order pizza from Milano's and have it delivered to England's Fine Furniture.

"That way poor Herbie won't have to close up the store while he runs out to grab some lunch," Mary explained. "Between the murder and his nightly encounters of the third kind, he's almost afraid to poke his head out the door. He only feels safe at the store. That's why he spends so much time there. Denny is lucky to have him as an employee. Herbie is a hard worker and is as honest as the day is long. Unlike some people I know, he doesn't fib, not even about what you call his nocturnal activities."

"Okay, you've made your point. Here, use my cell and order what you want, my treat." Little did I know how much Herbie Waddlemeyer liked pizza but I was about to find out. Apparently, neither the murder nor his nightly abductions by aliens had dulled Herbie's appetite. Twenty minutes later, the three of us were sharing an extra-large, stuffed-crust pizza from Milano's in Mary's office at England's Fine Furniture.

"Mmmm," Herbie hummed as he helped himself to the last slice of pizza after checking to be sure that Mary and I'd had our fill, "this is the best meal I've eaten all week. It's a heck of a lot better than the one I had at Leo's Bar and Grill last Saturday afternoon." He then went on to describe in detail the awful lunch he'd had that day.

I have to admit that I wasn't paying much attention to what Herbie had consumed at the greasy spoon located at the far end of Seville. Hardly anyone in town frequents the place and the only things that seem to draw any customers are Leo's late hours and liquor license. Curious as to why Herbie, a known teetotaler, chose to eat at the dumpy bar and grill, I asked him. His answer was even more astounding than his tales of alien abductions.

"Well, after I delivered a bedroom suite to Doc Parker's nephew, young Dr. Peter Parker and his bride, at their cottage out on Old Railway Road, it was lunchtime so I thought I'd stop and eat at that buffet restaurant off the interstate, but I got lost and ended up at Leo's. Like everyone else in town, I never heard a good word about the place so I was about to make a U-turn out of the parking lot," said Herbie as he paused to take a drink from his can of soda, "but with the way the lot's set up, I had to pull the truck around the back to make the swing. That's when I decided to try my luck with Leo's for lunch."

Herbie wasn't making a whole lot of sense, at least not to me but with Mary it was a different story. When I asked, with only a sliver of edge in my voice, what in God's name did making a difficult U-turn have to do with his decision to throw caution to the wind and eat in Leo's hellhole, it was Mary who enlightened me.

"Because," Mary said calmly and slowly as though she were dealing with a complete nincompoop (me, not Herbie), "he obviously saw something when he swung the truck around the back of Leo's that caused him to change his mind about the place not being up to Martha Stewart's standards. Isn't that right, Herbie?"

"Right," he replied, his owl-like eyes open wide in amazement at Mary's perception, "although I don't think I've ever had the pleasure of meeting your friend, Miz Stewart. Does she live here in town?"

"Oh my stars, no. Martha Stewart is that woman on television who knows all there is to know when it comes to food, even to what kind of flowers you should have on your table when you serve it. One time she made the cutest little . . ."

Unable to take it one more minute, I threatened to dump what was left of my ginger ale down the front of Mary's new blue silk blouse that cost forty-nine dollars (on sale, no less) if she didn't shut up about Martha Stewart. Turning to the quivering Herbie, I told him he had less than ten seconds to live if he didn't tell me exactly what had caused him to change his mind about eating at Leo's.

Less than five seconds later, I learned that Herbie had spotted Stuart Goodenough and Bambi Eastwood going into the back-room bar area via the rear door entrance.

"I figured if a rich lady like Miz Eastwood and a big
shot like Mr. Goodenough thought Leo's was an okay place
to go for lunch, then it was good enough for the likes of
me. I drove the truck back round the front, parked it and
went in through the main door that leads into the restaurant part. I didn't see anybody around except the waitress,
who told me that there was a couple of out-of-town swells,
a stocky guy and a big blond gal, who came in right before
me. She said that they were in the back-room bar where
they were eating and drinking like there was no tomorrow.
Not being a drinking man," Herbie added sanctimoniously,
"I steered clear of the back room and ate in the front part
of the place. When I was leaving, I could hear Miz Eastwood laughing. I don't know if you've ever noticed, she's
got a pretty distinctive laugh."

I was tempted to make a caustic comment regarding
Bambi's "distinctive laugh" but being more interested in
the timeline than getting off a clever line, I let the opportunity pass. Instead, I asked Herbie when all of this took
place. I suspected that the remains of food noted in Dr.
Loo's autopsy report came from Stuart's luncheon date
with Bambi Eastwood at Leo's. It would help my investigation if I could pin down the time.

"The way I figure it," said Herbie, using his fingertips to
tap the top of his large, round head as if to jump start his
brain, "it must have been sometime after twelve seein' that
I made the delivery to the cottage at noon on the dot and
then wasted about fifteen minutes to maybe a half hour
trying to find that all-you-can-eat buffet place off the interstate."

With the question answered to his satisfaction, the furniture store's star employee, the "honest as the day is long"
Herbie then began a lengthy, detailed description of his
self-diagnosed bout with food poisoning, courtesy of Leo's.
Cutting him short, I thanked Herbie for the info regarding
Bambi and Stuart. I was about to invite Mary to tag along
with me for an afternoon interview with Biddy McFarland
and her mother, Vilma Beatty, when Denny's unexpected

arrival brought my day of investigating to a screeching halt.

Upon hearing that Denny had dropped Charlie off at Kettle Cottage, I headed for home and husband. I didn't want to press my luck with another tall tale of spending time visiting nonexisting, potential clients and I surely wasn't about to confess to Charlie that once again I was sticking my nose where, in his and Matt's opinion, it didn't belong.

Chapter twenty

꙳

Before going into the house I had the good sense to check my cell phone for messages. Not wanting to be interrupted while questioning Arthur Kraft, I'd turned it off and had forgotten to turn it back on. I had three messages and they were all from JR telling me to call her back on her cell phone ASAP. Wasting no time, I punched in her number while mentally kicking myself for being so forgetful.

She answered on the first ring, a sure sign that either the baby was sleeping, Matt was home, or something was wrong. I was right about all three things.

"Mother, I hope you're sitting down," JR said in a voice barely above a whisper, "'cause I've got bad news." Not waiting for an answer from me, she continued, "I can't confirm Amanda's alibi."

"Oh jeez, just when I was on a roll or thought I was," I sadly admitted to my daughter. "I'll tell you all about it after you tell me what happened with Amanda's alibi."

"I'll make it quick before Matt discovers that I'm in the pantry and not upstairs checking on the baby. There's no Althea to be found. She walked out on Monday and nobody has seen her since. I tried to get her home phone number but the salon manager claims she never had it. Same story with the address. When I asked for the elusive Althea's last name, it turns out to be Smith. Do you have any idea how many Smiths are in the Indianapolis telephone book and the surrounding suburbs?"

Before I could answer, JR hurried on. "I then asked the manager to check the customer list for Saturday. It seems that the list, along with Althea, is nowhere to be found. Uh-oh, Matt's calling for me. Talk to you later."

Tucking the tiny phone into my purse, I got out of the van and tried to put a smile on my face as I opened the Dutch door and stepped into the kitchen of Kettle Cottage, where I was greeted by the perpetually grinning Mickey Mouse telephone, a pooch with the right moniker, and a grumpy husband.

"Well, well, if it isn't the Marx Brothers—Harpo, Chico, and Groucho," I said in a droll voice. "Let me put my purse away and then you can tell me all about your day at the races." My witty reference to the comedic trio and one of their best films was wasted on the Disney icon telephone, the purebred Keeshond, and most of all on my Prince Charming—the out-of-sorts Charlie.

"Would you believe that the sprinklers are all screwed up and the course is virtually flooded? No carts, not even the kind you pull will be allowed until the course dries out, that's how bad it is out there," Charlie grumbled.

"So how did you and Denny spend the morning? I know that you didn't get home until a few minutes ago."

"We took a ride over to the mall in Springvale to check out the sale on golf clubs at Nevada Bob's Sporting Goods, where we ran into Harry Eastwood," Charlie said, absent-mindedly rubbing the frown line on his forehead. "The guy was picking up the clubs he'd ordered when he was in there last Saturday afternoon. Being a lefty and a scratch golfer to boot, he said it was well worth the time and money he spent getting a great set of clubs with decent grips."

"Interesting," I remarked, wondering if Harry East-wood was aware of the fact that while he was checking out irons, woods, and putters on Saturday, Bambi Eastwood was at Leo's checking in with Stuart Goodenough.

Maybe the seemingly easygoing Harry wasn't actually as easygoing as he seemed. Being a wealthy man, he could have hired someone to do the deed for him. The only thing wrong with that theory was that it didn't work if Harry didn't know about Bambi and Stuart meeting on the sly or did know and didn't care. Or perhaps Harry had Stuart killed because he discovered that Stuart had helped him-self to the funds earmarked for flipping expenses. Or maybe Bambi bumped off the smooth-talking Stuart because he was cheating on her with Amanda Little.

I also reminded myself that I only had Arthur Kraft's word that he was out making deliveries Saturday after-noon. Even if that proved to be the case, I reasoned si-lently, Arthur could have made an unscheduled stop at the Semple house. Maybe he killed Stuart as payback for the con man's less-than-gallant plan of getting money from Amanda. I was sure that Amanda shared every word of the overheard conversation with the lovesick florist.

Nor could I eliminate Ben Kind or Duke Demarco as suspects, especially since their alibi was about as believ-able as the reports of Elvis being alive and stocking shelves at a Kmart Super Center somewhere north of Memphis and east of Las Vegas. Both the moneylender and the gen-eral contractor demonstrated their animosity toward Stuart when the men had individually confronted him about his dubious ethics, methods of operating, and missing funds. Ben was fearful of having his reputation ruined via his as-sociation with Stuart and Duke was angry about the money owed to him. In my book, fear and/or anger equaled mo-tive.

My head was starting to hurt. I had too many suspects with too many reasons for ending Stuart Goodenough's life. Reaching for the extra-strength Tylenol, I turned the kettle on for tea, two things that were tangible signs of my overloaded state of mind.

Never one to miss an opportunity, Charlie hit me with the news that he'd purchased a very expensive putter from Nevada Bob's. When he saw that I was in no shape to object, he was back to being his charming self. He insisted that I take the Tylenol, skip the tea, and go take a nap. He sealed the deal with a kiss and a promise to take me out to dinner at Giant Joe's Steak House located in Bard's Valley, a suburb of Indianapolis and Matt's old stomping grounds before he met JR.

"You go upstairs and have a good, long sleep. I promise I'll wake you up in plenty of time for you to get ready, sweetheart. Oh, and how about if I ask JR and Matt to join us? I think they both could use a night out, don't you?"

Assuring Charlie that it would indeed please me to have dinner with the Cusaks, I kicked off my shoes, plopped down on the four-poster bed, and covered myself with the crazy quilt comforter. The minute that my throbbing head hit the array of soft, buttery yellow and candy apple red accent pillows, the Tylenol kicked in. Before drifting off to the Land of Nod, I wondered if perhaps I'd run into an unsolvable puzzle—one that had too many pieces just as I had too many suspects. It would be interesting to hear what, if anything, Matt had to say about his investigation into the death of a scoundrel.

When Charlie woke me up with the news that I had a whole ten minutes to pull myself together for our dinner date with JR and Matt, I nearly fell out of bed.

"Ten minutes?" I protested, struggling to reenter the world of the living. "For your information, chum, it takes me longer than that to get ready to take out the garbage."

If I'd had the time, I might've also bemoaned the fact that while my closet was as bare as Mother Hubbard's cupboard, the laundry chute had enough clothes stuffed in it to clothe the naked of the earth and then some.

Ruefully aware that I would be dining in the outfit I'd

slept in, I sent up a quick prayer to St. Jude, the patron saint of hopeless causes, asking that the lighting in Giant Joe's be soft and forgiving. A fast pass with a brush, along with the red scrunchy to reel in my runaway hairdo, a slash of lipstick, and a smidgen of blush and I was about as ready as could be expected under the circumstances. As my husband (who looked like he belonged on the cover of *GQ* magazine) escorted me to the car, he had the good sense not to comment on my now saggy, baggy, green chenille jumpsuit. Had he been foolish enough to do so, I would have had my own motive for murder with the dapper Charlie as my victim.

Thirty-five minutes later, we arrived at the restaurant where Matt and JR were waiting for us in the bar. In spite of it being a weekday, the popular albeit expensive place was wall-to-wall with people waiting to be seated for dinner. The bar was as dim as a church confessional for which I was most thankful.

"I've got our name in for a table in the dining room but I told the hostess, Millie, that if push comes to shove, we don't mind eating in a booth right here in the bar," Matt said, relinquishing his seat at the crowded bar to me and putting me within whispering distance of the already seated JR.

Because our husbands were standing within earshot, JR and I kept our conversation broad and general, avoiding the subject of my investigation into Seville's latest murder. When the bartender switched the television channel from CNN Headline News to ESPN, the sports channel, I finally had the opportunity to catch JR up on what I'd learned from interviewing Arthur Kraft, the unplanned run-in with the Kinds, and sharing a pizza with Herbie and Mary down at the furniture store. With Charlie and Matt totally engrossed in film clips and commentary on every sport ever played since the dawn of mankind, JR and I were free to talk about anything we wanted to without fear of being overheard by our husbands.

"With so many suspects having so many motives for

killing the guy, it's a wonder that they didn't band together to commit the crime," remarked JR.

"Bite your tongue, missy. I've already got enough on my plate without having to deal with a real-life Agatha Christie mystery."

"Sorry, Mom, but you're going to have to run that by me again. What do you mean? What Agatha Christie mystery?" asked JR. Even though it was pretty noisy in the bar, I could hear the bewilderment in my daughter's voice.

"And I thought I raised you better than that," I said with a smirk, "I'm referring to one of her best mysteries, *Murder on the Orient Express*."

I was in the middle of an elaborate comparison between Christie's work of fiction and the very real mystery that I was trying my best to solve when the hostess announced that our table was ready.

While it was true about the table being ready, the same could not be said for me, especially when I realized that we were about to be shown to a large table in the center of the brightly lit dining room. Thinking fast, I slipped Millie a ten-spot and discreetly rolled my eyes in the direction of a tiny table for four in a pillar-hidden corner of the room.

Barely missing a step, the forty-something hostess bypassed the center table and led us to the remote corner. With a megawatt smile, she deposited four oversized menus on top of the undersized table and issued the standard command for us to enjoy our meal before disappearing like a thief in the night.

By the time Charlie and Matt managed to squeeze past the pillars and into their chairs, the handsome Carlos, our server for the evening, had seen to it that JR and I were comfortably seated. With great flair, he snapped open two of the four napkins on the table and presented one to JR and one to me. As with the seating, Charlie and Matt struggled for room when they unrolled the remaining two napkins.

In spite of the bad accommodations, we had a terrific meal and great service, thanks to Carlos, who hovered over the four of us like a bald eagle guarding his nest. Because of this, our conversation was limited to small talk and no one brought up the subject of Seville's latest murder or Matt's investigation of the crime. About as close as we got to the subject was when, after checking his watch, Matt announced that he and JR were calling it a night.

"Oh," I said to him, trying to sound more motherly than nosy, "what a shame. We were having such a nice visit, but I suppose you have a busy day tomorrow being in the middle of a murder investigation and all."

"That's for sure," said Matt with a grin. "I promised the school principal, Mr. Tuttle, I'd be there with Sid no later than nine. It's career day and thanks to Kerry and Kelly, we're going to be the main speakers."

"So much for gleaning info out of Matt," I remarked to JR as we waited in the lobby of Giant Joe's while our husbands took care of the bill.

"Yeah, but all and all, it was a nice evening. The only complaint I have is that the table was on the dinky side and the seating kind of tight, especially for Pops and Matt. For a minute there, I thought we were going to have to call the fire department to either remove our husbands or those pillars."

JR and I were still giggling about Charlie, Matt, and the pillars when the two men caught up with us. With three valets on duty, it didn't take long for our cars to come to a zooming halt under the canopy. Since other people were waiting for their vehicles, Charlie and I kept our good-byes to Matt and JR short and sweet. It wasn't until Charlie made the turn onto the interstate that it dawned on me what JR had whispered in my ear when she kissed me on my cheek: "Mom, do you know that you're wearing two different shoes? A black loafer and a brown moccasin."

At last I had some hard evidence. Unfortunately it was against Charlie, whose crime was assuming that ten minutes was "plenty of time to get ready," which he compounded by not noticing my mismatched footwear. But when he reached across the seat of the car and gave my hand a squeeze, I made the decision to forgive and forget. Like my latest foray into Matt's business, some things were best left unsaid.

Chapter twenty-one

❧

The following morning, I was busy feeding the washer and dryer in an effort to replenish my exhausted wardrobe. I wanted to at least look neat and clean, if not fashionable, when I dropped in on Biddy McFarland and her mother, Vilma Beatty. Although the two women weren't high on my list of people I needed to interview about the murder, I still wanted to talk to them. Perhaps if I got them gabbing about the murder, it might trigger something that they had forgotten or withheld from the police because it seemed trivial or inconsequential at the time. I stopped long enough to phone JR. I was going to ask her if she and Kris would like to tag along but as usual, my timing was bad.

"Mother, whatever it is that you want will have to wait," she informed me in an uptight voice. "I'm in the middle of getting Kerry and Kelly off to school. They were so busy bickering over whose backpack was whose that they missed the bus. I'm trying to get myself and the baby dressed so I can drive them to school. I'll call you back." Click.

Thirty minutes later, I was in the middle of feeding yet another load of wash into the aging Maytag when the phone rang. Expecting the caller to be JR, I was momentarily thrown off-kilter by a familiar, creepy voice asking to speak with Mrs. Hastings. "Speaking," I said. "What can I do for you, Mrs. Daggert?"

"The master said to tell you that the report is ready and you can pick it up when you come here for lunch. Twelve sharp. The two of you will be dining in his office. I'll set up two trays. Don't be late and don't be expecting anything fancy. Do you think you can remember all that?"

"Yes, and Mrs. Daggert," I said in the most sickening sweet voice I could muster, "I want to thank you for the call and your gracious invitation." If I thought I had bested the old crone, a throwback to the Dark Ages, I was wrong. She'd already hung up.

Handing the phone over to the mouse with the nonstop smile, I went back to feeding the old but dependable washing machine. Call me crazy but I like my appliances to look like appliances and that includes my kitchen phone and excludes Charlie's latest eBay purchase, the grinning Mickey.

Twenty minutes later the phone rang again. It was JR with the news that after dropping the twins off at school, she'd decided to drive over to the mall in Springvale for a day of shopping and goofing off with baby Kris.

When she asked what I'd called about, I claimed I'd forgotten and told her to chalk it up to my having a senior moment. I wasn't about to spoil her day of impromptu R and R with an invitation to participate in one of the more boring aspects of sleuthing—conducting interviews.

Although she didn't sound all that convinced with the senior moment excuse, JR did promise to be careful. I was ready to hang up when she reminded me that it was career day at the school. "Keep your fingers crossed that it goes well for Matt and Sid. Kids can be a tough audience and a bad reception from them could make a long day seem even longer."

"Long day? You mean Matt and Sid have to stay at school the entire day?" I said with a chuckle, picturing the two decorated police officers spending their time dealing with the three Rs, food fights in the cafeteria, and playground bullies.

"No, of course not. When they finish with their career day speeches, they plan on driving out to Castle Hills to check out Stuart's penthouse apartment. And before you ask, he didn't say what he expected to find. Listen, Mom, Kris is starting to fuss. I'll talk to you later. Bye-bye."

With JR and the baby no longer part of my own plans for the day, I decided that I would drop in on Biddy and Vilma after, rather than before, my business lunch with Horatio. The change in plans gave me more than enough time to finish the wash, take a leisurely shower, put on my makeup, and pick out something nice to wear, including shoes that matched.

It was while I was in the shower (a place where I do some of my best thinking) that I reviewed the case against Amanda Little. She had the motive but did she have the means? Maybe, maybe not. Did someone steal her key and chain? Maybe, maybe not. And was there really an Althea who could verify her alibi? On this third "maybe, maybe not" I made a couple of important decisions. The first one was that if I couldn't figure out who the real murderer was pretty soon, I was going to advise Amanda to get in touch with Jerry Dobbs, the best criminal defense attorney in Indianapolis.

Jerry was and is the closest thing I have to a sibling. When his parents were killed in an auto accident, he came to live with me and my parents. Jerry assumed the role of big brother and I adored him. I still do.

The other decision I came to was never to buy an olive-and-herb-scented shampoo again. Not only did it sting my eyes, it left my hair smelling like a relish tray.

Chapter twenty-two

Smartly dressed in a freshly laundered, black-and-white cotton pantsuit and shoes that matched, I arrived at Horatio's on time, where, as promised, lunch was ready and waiting in his office. Even though Mrs. Daggert had warned me not to expect anything fancy, she might have warned me that we were having haggis, a Scottish dish and one that I knew nothing about and had never tasted. The old crone seemed to take great delight in telling me how hard she'd worked mincing the liver, heart, and lungs of the sheep; adding in the oatmeal, spices, and onions; and then cooking the mixture in the animal's stomach. By the time she was done with sharing the recipe, I'd lost my appetite, which I suspected was exactly what the housekeeper from hell had in mind all along.

When Mrs. Daggert returned later to check on how we were progressing with the meal, I don't think I fooled her (or Horatio) with my claim to have recently converted to vegetarianism. It wasn't exactly a lie. After my unexpected introduction to the Scottish delicacy, I was seriously considering doing just that.

"Is there anything else I can get for you, Mr. Bordeaux, before I return to the kitchen?" inquired Mrs. Daggert, deliberately turning her back to me and my virtually untouched meal and acting as though Horatio was the only person in the room other than herself.

"No, not unless Mrs. Hastings would like something?" Horatio had made short work of his serving of haggis and was sniffing the air like a dog at a backyard barbecue. "I say, is that apple pie I smell? Perhaps our guest would care for some dessert and maybe a cup of your excellent coffee."

"Sorry, sir, the coffee grinder isn't working and that smell is a new air freshener I picked up at the market the other day. Now, if you will excuse me, I'd better be getting back to the kitchen. If you need anything, you know where to find me."

"As long as you're going that way, Mrs. Daggert, would you mind taking my tray?" I piped up. "Since I really didn't touch much of the haggis, perhaps you would like to save some of it for your evening meal."

With a harrumph as she looked at me and a grunt as she lifted the tray, Mrs. Daggert made her exit. Once the housekeeper had disappeared down the hallway, Horatio wheeled himself over to the now-open sliding doors. Peeking out like a small boy to see if the coast was clear, he then wheeled himself back into the room and closed the doors. Expecting him to go directly to his desk, I was surprised when he brought the wheelchair to a halt in front of the dark oak, richly carved highboy, where, with a touch of his hand, the cabinet door opened. Reaching inside, Horatio removed a bottle of Webber's Bay Merlot along with a crystal wine goblet and a small bag of pretzels.

"I can vouch for the wine but I'm afraid I can't do the same for the freshness of the pretzels," he said, pouring out a glass of the dark red wine and dumping the salty snack into a nearby empty crystal candy dish. "You don't think I bought that story about your being a vegetarian, do you? Help yourself, Jeannie, I know you're hungry."

Then, because he knows me so well, he produced an ashtray, flipped a switch for the overhead fan, and pushed open the trio of tall windows that took up most of the wall behind his massive, dark oak desk. Like the man himself, the entire room was warm and inviting. I've always felt at ease in Horatio's office/study with its book-lined shelves, stone fireplace, and handsome, brown leather furniture. I also was proud that Designer Jeans had turned the room into a workable and handicapped-friendly space that looked as great as it functioned.

A half a bowl of pretzels accompanied by a couple of healthy sips of wine followed by a cigarette and I was ready to get down to the business of reading Horatio's report. Finding nothing of real interest regarding Harry Eastwood, Ben Kind, Duke Demarco, Arthur Kraft, or Amanda Little, I spent most of my time on the Stuart Goodenough and Bambi Eastwood portion of the report.

The closest the career con artist, Stuart Goodenough, had ever come to living on the right side of the law was the time he'd spent in the air force during the early 1980s. While stationed in his home state of Nevada, he went AWOL enough times that it became obvious that Stuart didn't have the right stuff. Upon receiving an early discharge from the air force, he hopped the first bus for Las Vegas, where he devoted his time to scamming people out of their money.

It was at one of the seedier gentlemen's clubs that Stuart met Bambi Lake, a wannabe showgirl turned stripper. They married and divorced twice before realizing that they were better suited as business partners than marriage partners. Their most lucrative scam was one that involved Bambi giving private lap dances (and more) to inebriated conventioneers who'd come to Vegas to conduct business as usual in the day and raise hell at night before returning to the wife and kiddies back home in small town America.

A few drops of gamma hydroxybutyric acid (GHB) in a drink and the sucker never knew the fun he had with the gal who'd danced her way into his bed until the next day. That's when he woke up with a pounding headache, no memory of what had taken place in the hotel room, and a note on the dresser informing him that unless he paid big bucks for the tape of his sexual escapade with Bambi, it would be mailed to his home and a copy to his place of employment. Bambi and Stuart were busted when they tangled with a swinger from California who'd helped the police set up a sting operation.

Stuart got three years, unlike Bambi, who received a pat on the fanny (the judge was a regular at the gentlemen's club) and six months' probation. It was while Stuart was serving his sentence and Bambi was servicing the judge that she met and married the recently divorced and very lonely Harry Eastwood.

The young stripper and the wealthy, retired plastic manufacturer might have lived happily ever after but for two events that changed everything. The first was that after only eighteen months, Stuart Goodenough was released due to prison overcrowding. The second was that Harry sold his Vegas condo and moved with his young bride to Seville. While Harry was busy setting up a new life with his new wife in Seville, Indiana, Stuart headed for Castle Hills, Indiana, and Bambi, having figured out a new way to fleece people out of money, especially the new groom, the rich Mr. Eastwood.

Using the perfectly legal practice of house flipping as bait and passing himself off as a successful real estate broker/experienced flipper, Stuart convinced others to invest in his flip project—the Semple manse. While the little group waited for a return on their investment, the con man was padding his pockets with the fee he'd received for using Ben Kind's mortgage company, kickbacks from various suppliers and subcontractors, and dipping into the construction fund via fake invoices.

"Jeez, this reads like a bad novel or a script for a B movie," I cried, clutching the file to my chest. "Unfortunately, as fascinating and informative as I found it to be, it doesn't help me point the finger of suspicion away from Amanda Little."

"Maybe," suggested Horatio, returning the wine and what was left of the pretzels to their hiding place, "you should look at the report as another piece of the puzzle and not the solution. Give it a chance to fit in and I believe that you'll find the right time and place to use the information I've gathered. But first, you've got to use your brain and trust your instincts. If you do, then I'm sure that you'll solve the puzzle. You always do."

I gathered up my things, including the report, gave Horatio a kiss on his chubby, bearded cheek, and made my exit.

Chapter twenty-three

✦

The distance between Horatio's place and the McFarlands' Victorian was a relatively short one, but it was long enough for me to mull over Horatio's advice and encouragement. His ability to blend the two elements is part of the reason why I have such respect for the man.

Arriving at my destination, I was still thinking of Horatio's words of wisdom as I pressed the doorbell of the old Victorian, failing to notice the newly installed intercom set up on the opposite side of the front door frame.

"Who's ringing that bell?" demanded the scratchy but far from timid voice. The readily identifiable, disembodied voice was that of Vilma Beatty, Biddy's elderly mother. "Speak up and identify yourself. It's not all that complicated. Press the button and talk into that thingamabob right in front of your nose. Don't make me come down there or you'll be sorry. I'm not big but I'm armed and mean."

"Mrs. Beatty, it's Jean Hastings from Designer Jeans. I was in the neighborhood and thought I might visit with you and Bid . . ." Catching myself in time, I managed to spit out Biddy's given name of Bridget. Suspecting that the elderly Vilma was home alone, I apologized for disturbing her and said I would return some other day, adding that I would be sure to phone ahead of time.

"Hogwash. You stay right where you are," commanded the feisty Vilma, "and as soon as I find the right button, I'll buzz you in."

A few minutes later, after complying with her demand that I join her for high tea in her second-floor private suite, Vilma and I were enjoying a steaming pot of herbal tea, freshly baked buttery scones, and Biddy's homemade cinnamon apple butter. Perched on her scooter, which she'd parked next to the tea cart, Vilma looked both pleased with herself, the cart's contents, and her unexpected company.

In view of Biddy's absence (according to Vilma, her daughter was spending the afternoon playing bridge with friends) I decided that it would've been tacky on my part to question the elderly woman about what she might have observed on the day of Stuart's murder. I did my best to stick to my decision but it wasn't easy thanks to Vilma.

Reveling in her role of hostess, the old lady took charge of the conversation, filling even the tiniest lull with stories from her days as a young girl growing up in Seville. It was in the middle of one such story that she mentioned the sad saga of Edith Semple.

"It's a pity that Edith never had the chance to marry that young artist. The closest she ever got to being his bride is when she posed for him in her wedding finery. The portrait was to be his wedding present to her." Vilma sighed. "That's how I'll always remember Edith. Young and slender, long golden hair and standing in the yard. That's why when I saw Danny Semple," she said, using the family name rather than the rocker's stage name, "last Saturday afternoon in the yard next door, he reminded me so much of Edith. She wasn't very tall or robust, either."

"Are you telling me that you actually saw him here in Seville last Saturday afternoon?" I sputtered, nearly choking on the hot tea and stunned by her comment. Either Vilma was having a senior moment or I was and my money was on Vilma. Or at least it was until she explained everything to me in detail.

"Bridget had just come up to help me into bed for my afternoon nap when I looked out the window and saw the young man walking around the Semple backyard with a container of some sort. It might have been a can of soda, at least that's what it looked like to me, but Bridget, who saw him, too, said it looked like a container of flower food. Far be it for me to argue the point seeing that Bridget's the gardener in the family. That husband of hers wouldn't be caught dead pushing a lawn mower."

Eager to keep the elderly woman's focus on what she saw and not on her son-in-law's propensity to avoid physical activity of any kind, I nudged her back on track by asking if she knew what time it was when she spotted the intruder. Even though I was aware that he'd been booked into Indianapolis for a two-week gig, the news that Danny, if that's who it was, had been in Seville on the day of Stuart's murder came as a complete surprise.

"Bridget always makes me take a nap at two o'clock every day except Wednesday even when I'm not tired. Thank the good Lord for that bridge club of hers otherwise I'd be in bed counting sheep right now instead of having my very own company." Vilma popped the last portion of the cinnamon apple butter–slathered scone into her mouth and smiled. I could only hope that her memory was as good as her appetite.

"Was Mr. Goodenough in the yard during that time?" I asked, not knowing Stuart's exact whereabouts at two o'clock. For all I knew, he could've been still eating and drinking in Leo's Bar and Grill with the laughing Bambi at the time Vilma claimed to have seen the bad boy of hard metal rock walking around the flip property's yard.

"Not as far as I could tell. I don't think that Mr. Goodenough came outside after being dropped off at the front door of the house a few minutes earlier by that new gal in town with the silly name. You'd think she would have dropped him off at his car. It was parked right down the street. More tea, Jean, dear?" inquired Vilma before transferring what was left of the contents of the pot into her cup.

"No, thank you, Mrs. Beatty," I answered, "and I believe the name you're trying to think of is Bambi."

"That's right. Bambi. Now I ask you have we as a society lost all sense of propriety? Imagine, naming someone after a forest creature and a fictional one at that," sniffed Vilma Beatty, pointing her turned-up nose toward the sitting room's high ceiling. From where I was sitting, I had the opportunity to study the elderly woman's profile. I couldn't help but notice the strong resemblance between mother and daughter not only in attitude but physically as well despite the age and weight difference.

"Did the person that you saw stay in the yard or go into the house?" I held my breath as I waited for the answer.

"Into the house. Went through the French doors on the side. The doors lead into the dining room but maybe that got changed with all the dad-blamed construction," Vilma said before going on her own quest for information. "Granted, Edith wasn't the greatest neighbor but she certainly was the quietest. With the murder and all, I can't help but wonder what's going to happen to the place. I don't suppose there's any chance of that Danny person buying it back, do you?"

I gave her an honest answer when I told her that I doubted it. I also admitted that I didn't know myself what was going to happen to the property. What I didn't say was that I was more concerned about Amanda Little's fate than that of an old Victorian house. If what Vilma Beatty saw was accurate and could be verified, then Amanda Little, alibi or no alibi, was one step closer to a future that didn't include standing trial for murdering Stuart Goodenough.

The glass-domed gold clock sitting on a shelf in the bookcase delicately chimed the hour, a gentle reminder that it was time for me to leave. In spite of my protest, Vilma

Beatty insisted on taking the elevator ride with me to the
first floor. Seated on her electric scooter, she was about to
lead the way to the elevator when Biddy McFarland unexpectedly walked into the room.

Although her eyes had locked in on me, Biddy addressed her comments to her mother. "Well, this is a surprise. Why didn't you tell me that you were expecting
company or was it a surprise to you as well? I don't recall
receiving any phone call or even a note about arranging for
a visit, especially on a Wednesday, my bridge club day."

Looking more like a senior member of the British royal
family than a member of America's middle class, it was
obvious that Biddy McFarland was not pleased upon finding that her authority as keeper of the gate had been
usurped by her mother. Half expecting to be arrested or
shown the door by the palace guards, I apologized pro-
fusely for what Biddy considered a complete lack of good
manners on my part and was about to make a run for it
when Vilma intervened on my behalf.

"I think I've heard enough twiddle-twaddle for one day.
Bridget, let me remind you that my name is still on the title
of this house, not yours or what's-his-name's. I'll see who I
want when I want and without checking first with you or
anyone else. Now, if you have any manners of your own,
you'll see my guest to the front door. I'm going to my bedroom to take a nap. Call me when supper's ready."

Expertly maneuvering the scooter past the red-faced,
openmouthed Biddy, Vilma Beatty gave me a wink before
disappearing into her bedroom and closing the door with a
resounding thud. "And don't come in here to tuck me in. I
like my privacy," shouted Vilma loud enough to be heard
by the two of us as we stood inside the elevator waiting for
it to take us to the floor below.

Chapter twenty-four

By the time the short ride was over and Biddy escorted me to the front door, she'd pulled herself together and was the one doing the apologizing.

"Please excuse my mother. As you can tell, age has caught up with her. That's part of the reason I have to be so strict about visitors," said Biddy, her voice dripping in a condescending sweetness. "I'm sure you understand, Jean, seeing what's happened to your own dear mother. I understand that you finally had to place her in a nursing home in southern California. I guess when the mind is gone, it doesn't matter to the poor dears where their last days are spent. What a shame. Your mother was such a gifted piano teacher. I suppose now she doesn't even remember how to play."

I was tempted to inform Biddy that these days my widowed mother does all her playing (which has nothing to do with a piano) in the ocean on a surfboard, that is when she and her cousin Moira aren't off whale watching, saving California's sharks, or feeding the slots in a Las Vegas casino. Trying to catch my mother at home in the beachfront

condo she shares with Moira is like trying to catch a
greased pig. It can be done, but it's not easy.

Since Biddy had brought up the subject of Vilma's di-
minishing mental abilities, I told her what the elderly
woman had to say about seeing someone whom she identified as Danny Semple in the yard next door on the afternoon of the murder.

"That's a perfect example of what I'm talking about. I
was standing right next to Mother and saw everything she
did but her version of the incident is so wrong, it breaks my
heart," said Biddy.

"Are you telling me that your mother didn't see someone creeping around the outside of the Semple house last
Saturday?"

"What I'm telling you, Jean, is the same thing I told
Rollie Stevens and later your son-in-law, Matt Cusak. It
wasn't a young man that my mother saw that afternoon, it
was a woman and that woman was Amanda Little. I wish
with all my heart that it wasn't her but it was. It was
Amanda Little, I'd bet my life on it." Biddy was adamant
and was not about to consider that perhaps she, and not
Vilma, was the one who was mistaken.

"What do you think triggered your mother's faulty interpretation of the incident? She seemed so sure that she
saw a man, and that man was Danny." I was beginning to
think that if I had to wait much longer to light up a cigarette, I might go a bit dotty myself.

"Newspapers and television. Mother's read every word
that Hilly Murrow has written about the Semple house
murder. Her column on Monday included a photo biogra-
phy of the entire Semple family. Once she saw that young
man's picture, he's all Mother wants to talk about. She says
he's the spitting image of Edith. She's almost driven poor
Gordy crazy. And it hasn't helped that all the TV stations
out of Indy are running ads for the young man's Indianapolis concert," said Biddy. "From what I've been told about
his particular style of entertainment, he belongs in a mental institution or a rehab facility and not on a stage."

Ignoring Biddy's comments regarding the heavy metal rocker's stage act, I made the remark that since neither her own nor her mother's eyewitness account could be verified, it was possible that they were both mistaken.

Biddy McFarland shook her head in exasperation. "Unlike Mother, whose eyesight is getting as bad as her mind and thinks anyone wearing trousers is a man, I'm not fooled by all the unisex clothing favored by today's young adults. I know the difference and I know who I saw. I saw a woman dressed in tight-fitting white jeans with a matching jacket trimmed in gold. With her slim figure and mane of unnaturally bright, blond hair, she was pretty hard to miss. It was Amanda Little. There's no doubt about it whatsoever." If nothing else, Biddy was emphatic.

Recognizing Biddy's "gotcha" moment and taking a cue from a favorite saying among poker players about knowing when to fold, I thanked Biddy for her time and the information regarding Vilma's bouts with mental confusion and headed for home.

I returned to Kettle Cottage, where I was greeted by a hungry fuzz ball and her exhausted master. Apparently, playing eighteen holes of golf on a soggy course sans cart was too much even for someone like Charlie, who's generally quite hale and hearty.

Filling the pampered pooch's food bowl with a measured amount of Dandy Diet dog food, I tiptoed past the den where Charlie had fallen asleep and made my way upstairs to the master bedroom. Once there, I slipped out of my dressy outfit and into my favorite (and freshly laundered) black sweatshirt and pants.

Returning to the kitchen, I sat down at the table, where I enjoyed a can of soda, a cigarette, and the peace and quiet of my home. It had been quite a day and I had some serious thinking to do, mainly about Amanda Little and the growing mountain of evidence against her in the death of the con man, Stuart Goodenough.

Biddy McFarland, I reminded myself, was a gossip but she was not a liar. She genuinely liked Amanda and had no reason to fabricate a story that placed the real estate agent at the scene of the crime and within the time frame of the murder.

Using logic, I reasoned that if I were to make sense out of the information that was flooding my brain, I needed sustenance. I also had a feeling that Charlie was in need of some TLC. As does his twin sister, my husband associates TLC with food. Looking around the cozy room, I made the decision to make a meal that would satisfy both our needs.

Inspired by the Tuscan decor of my kitchen, I began with a menu of baked lasagna, salad greens tossed in vinegar and oil with grated Parmesan cheese and cherry tomatoes, crunchy crusted garlic bread, spumoni for dessert, and a bottle of Chianti. Once the cooking and salad making had been taken care of, I focused my attention on the atmosphere I wanted to create using only my imagination and items I had on hand.

First, I dressed the table in a mustard-colored bedsheet and slipped burgundy-colored pillow shams over the back of the chairs. To complement the two colors, I used an old, floral-print runner trimmed in citrus green fringe, draping it on angle across the middle of the table.

A fat, partially spent, red candle left over from Christmas took on a new look when set in a carnival glass compote dish that I placed in the center of the table.

Eating utensils rolled up in dinner-size, white paper napkins fastened with amethyst-colored ribbon, Fiesta dinnerware in hues of red, brown, and green, a cut-glass punch bowl filled with oranges and lemons, and two mismatched wineglasses completed the inviting, Italian countryside look.

There was only one more thing that needed to be done other than lighting the candle. Dashing up the stairs, I stepped in front of the bathroom vanity, ran a brush through my hair, applied a healthy dose of smoky-colored shadow to my eyelids, and dabbed a bit of vanilla extract behind my ears.

"All you hot lover boys out there, eat your hearts out," I gushed, imitating the seemingly ageless Italian actress Sophia Loren's sultry accent and striking a sexy pose as I checked out my image in the mirror. "Tonight, I belong only to my Charlie."

"If you really mean that, then I suggest we get started before either the lasagna or your ardor cools off."

"Charlie Hastings, shame on you for eavesdropping," I cried, pushing him out of the bathroom doorway and running down the stairs. "Last one to the table has to load the dishwasher." Although my challenge wasn't very romantic, it was effective.

When dinner was over, Charlie insisted I relax with a second glass of wine while he took care of clearing the table and loading the dishwasher. Later, I told him even though he lost the race, he won my heart. All in all it was a great evening.

Chapter twenty-five

The following morning, Thursday, I was up in time to pop a frozen breakfast in the microwave for Charlie before he had to leave to pick up Denny. The two were going to golf Springvale's municipal course. Despite having an early tee time, Charlie worried that the course would be extremely crowded, something that would make for a very long day. The long drive to Springvale, in Charlie's opinion, trumped sloshing down Sleepy Hollow's still mushy fairways.

"I have no idea what time I'll be home," Charlie said, accidentally on purpose dropping a morsel of sausage into the waiting mouth of our wide-bodied, tail-wagging food reservoir. "I'll try to call you when we're done but don't worry if you don't hear from me."

Reaching for his golf sweater on the back of the chair, he gave Pesty a good-bye pat and me a really, really nice farewell hug and kiss. "With nothing looming on Designer Jeans's schedule, why don't you and Mary take a trip to Chicago. Make it an overnighter. I'm sure Denny won't mind. The weather is perfect for a walk along the lake, lunch at Navy Pier, visiting the Art Institute or one of the museums. Or you could do some shopping on Michigan Avenue. They don't call it the Magnificent Mile for nothing."

"Hey, chum, you can't get rid of me as easily as that." I laughed as I helped myself to some grapefruit slices, thankful that a certain overfed bowwow never developed a taste for the mouth-puckering fruit. "You know me, I'll find something to do."

Charlie's handsome face took on a serious look. "That's what I'm afraid of," he mumbled more to himself than me, "once you've seen this morning's edition of the *Sentinel*."

"What in the world are you talking about?" I replied, looking around for the newspaper. For some reason that I couldn't fathom other than Charlie must have had a sudden attack of instant environmentalism, the newspaper had been deposited in the recycle bin before I even had a chance to glance at it. Plucking it out of the bin, I unfolded the newspaper and read the headline: Woman's Body Found in Castle Hills Condo.

Scrambling madly to find my reading glasses, I hardly acknowledged Charlie's mantra about minding my own business and not our son-in-law's. Fortunately, two things happened at once that allowed me to read the entire news article from first line to last without interruption—Charlie left the house and I found my glasses. I was wearing them. I'd forgotten that I'd put them on in order to read the microwave instructions on the frozen breakfast food package. Like the breakfast itself, the printing was miniscule.

Reading Hilly's article on Bambi's death (something that the reporter had decided was a suicide), I strongly suspected it contained more fiction than fact. I was in the process of digesting her version of the tragedy when the kitchen phone rang. It was my junior partner calling with the rest of the story.

"Whoa, slow down, JR. You're starting to sound like Alvin and the Chipmunks," I said, not wanting to miss a word of what she had to tell me.

"Sorry 'bout that. I've had all this info bottled up inside

since Matt came home last night. He and Sid were the ones who discovered her body and from what Matt says, it wasn't a pretty sight."

"Jeez, you mean you knew about Bambi's body being found in Stuart's penthouse and waited until this morning to call me? Why didn't you phone me last night?"

"At eleven o'clock? Come on, Mother, use your head. Nine times out of ten when the phone rings in your house that late Pops answers it. If he didn't think it was strange for me to be calling you so late, I'm sure as hell that Matt would have. Besides, Matt was so bushed when he got home, he really didn't say too much about it until this morning. Then I had to wait until he left for work and the twins went to school before I dared to call you."

JR had barely returned to telling me the where and when (the why and how had yet to be determined by the authorities) of Bambi's demise when the sound of an unhappy Kris drowned out any further conversation.

"Oh rats, I gotta go. Why don't you hop in the van and come over here? I've got more to tell you unless you want to wait on the phone while I see to Kris's needs, which include a bottle, a bath, a diaper change, some playtime, another diaper change, and if I'm lucky, a nap after breakfast."

"Stop. I'm getting tired just listening to you. Give me a few minutes to clean up and I'll be over," I said.

Throwing the few dishes from breakfast into the sink and giving the rest of the house "a lick and a promise" (an old expression favored by my mother), I filled Pesty's bowl with ice water and offered the spoiled fluff ball a diet doggy biscuit to tide her over until her next meal.

True to her breed, the little Keeshond showed her stubborn side and promptly rejected the rock-hard object. Holding out for something better, Pesty retreated to her favorite spot under the kitchen table, where she settled down for her morning nap.

"I'll be back in a little while," I said to the sulking, drowsy Kees as I made my way over to the closed and latched Dutch door. In spite of it being a mild, breezy morning, the kitchen was warm and stuffy. Thinking that both the room and the dog could do with a bit of fresh air, I unlocked the top part of the door, pulled it open, and found myself nose to nose with Mary.

"Jesus, Mary, and Joseph," I cried out, momentarily thrown by her unexpected appearance at the door, "you about scared me half to death! You really know how to surprise a person."

"Why? Because I happened to get ready before you? I thought we might have time for a bite before we leave," said Mary, handing me a box of Koffee Kabin assorted pastries.

Oblivious to my open mouth, Mary unlatched the bottom half of the door and stepped into the kitchen, where she was greeted by a suddenly revitalized Pesty. A Keeshond never forgets a visitor, especially someone like Mary, who always comes calling with a delicious treat in hand.

"I didn't bother picking up coffee. I thought you could make a pot, but I'll do it so you can finish getting ready."

"But I am ready." I protested, calling Mary's attention to the black sweatshirt and pants I'd thrown on when I rolled out of bed to make Charlie's breakfast. I count anything that has to be removed from its packaging as making a meal.

"Now, Gin, don't be offended but I hardly think that your choice in outfits is appropriate, if you know what I mean. Do you know what I'm saying?"

"No, I don't know what you mean and furthermore, I don't know what you've been saying since I found you on the back stoop. But as long as you're here, you are more than welcome to come along with me to JR's," I replied, giving up on trying to make sense out of the conversation, "and that goes for the box of Danish, too. I'm sure that she'll make us some coffee."

"My stars, is JR going with us to Chicago? Who's going to watch the baby? I hope it's Sally Birdwell," chirped

Mary, referring to the relatively young widow who operates a successful B and B next door to Kettle Cottage. "She has such a sweet way with everybody, including babies, and she's also very trustworthy."

"Wait a minute, Mary," I shouted loud enough to send a certain pudgy pooch running for cover under the table, "did your brother by any chance invite you to accompany me on a trip to Chicago?"

"Well, yes and no. When Charlie picked up Denny, he said that you were thinking about driving to Chicago and hesitant about asking me to go with. He said that you thought it was an imposition. That's when I made it clear that I would love to go. Charlie was holding his cell phone when he told me to go pack my things while he squared it with you," Mary said, sounding as confused as she looked. "He never mentioned anything about JR. Honestly, Gin, if this is strictly a mother-daughter trip, I'll stay home. In fact, I'll be more than happy to watch Kris. I love the little guy."

In an effort to minimize the damage done by Charlie's attempt to remove me from temptation (aka sleuthing) by sending me off to Chicago with his twin sister, I put the blame for the whole mixed-up mess on myself. I told Mary that I'd obviously missed Charlie's call because, as usual, I'd forgotten to turn on my cell phone or to check for messages after talking to JR on the kitchen phone, which happened to be the truth.

"So rather than drive to Chicago without you, JR and I decided to stay home," I said, which happened to be a big fat fib, yet if it spared Mary's feelings, it was worth it. I would deal with Charlie later. What really mattered was that Mary was ready, willing, and eager to trade a day of rubbernecking in the Windy City for a day of sleuthing in Seville when I insisted that she come along with me to JR's.

Armed with the box of pastries (minus the jelly doughnut that Mary hand-fed to an adoring Pesty) and with the best friend and sister-in-law anyone could ask for sitting in the passenger seat of the van, I headed for the house on Tall Timber Road with my own idea of R and R, which in this case meant real facts and real information pertaining to Bambi Eastwood's death. Unlike the *Sentinel*'s star reporter (and I use the term *star reporter* lightly), I don't believe in jumping to conclusions.

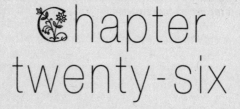Chapter twenty-six

"On the surface Bambi's death seems to be a suicide, although I find that hard to believe and even said so to Matt when he told me about finding her body on the living room floor of the penthouse. He was pretty vague about the time of death, which is understandable since the air conditioner was going full blast," said JR as she handed the baby a teething biscuit to munch on while he sat in his high chair. Kris had made short work of his soupy baby cereal breakfast and the biscuit was his reward. "It might very well be that Bambi took her own life since she didn't appear to have any defensive wounds, but that's something the medical examiner will have to determine.

"Harry Eastwood told Matt that Bambi had called him sometime late Tuesday afternoon. She said that she'd spent the day shopping in downtown Indy and before heading home she had to help a friend with a problem or something like that." JR paused long enough to move her chair out of Kris's food-tossing range. "According to Mr. Eastwood, that was the last time he spoke with his wife."

"Wasn't Harry suspicious? Did he ask her who this

friend was or what the problem was? I can't imagine telling your father something like that and getting away with it," I said, interrupting JR.

"I have no idea, Mom. Matt didn't fill in the blanks. From past experience, I wasn't about to put an end to our discussion by asking too many questions."

JR was right. I told her so and that I appreciated the information she'd managed to get out of the generally closed-mouthed Matt.

"Of course, since Castle Hills is out of Seville's jurisdiction, the medical examiner handling the autopsy won't be Dr. Loo," continued JR, giving me a look that warned me not to interrupt a second time. "Officially, Matt turned the entire matter over to the Castle Hills authorities, including the laptop computer containing Bambi's suicide note. In the note, she confesses to murdering Stuart Goodenough."

Listening intently to everything JR was saying, I keyed in on the word "officially" and brought it up when JR paused long enough to refill my coffee cup and make another pot of tea for herself and Mary.

"So if I'm reading you right, officially Matt is off the case but unofficially he's involved. Did he say why?" I asked.

"Oh, he kinda slid over that part when I asked him and I could tell that he didn't want to discuss it. But when I read the part out loud about what Hilly Murrow said in the *Sentinel* about Bambi's death being a suicide, he looked at me like I'd said something totally ridiculous."

Mary, who had been pretty quiet up until this point, brought up the fact that Hilly Murrow didn't mention anything about a note being found on the computer. "In fact, she didn't mention any note at all and toward the end of the article, she insinuated that suicide or not, Amanda Little was most likely responsible for Bambi Eastwood's death although she didn't say why or use Amanda's name."

"According to Matt, the authorities are keeping mum regarding the suicide note that was found on the computer because his investigation into Stuart Goodenough's murder is an ongoing one," JR said, scooping up the baby from the yucky mess that he'd made with the teething treat. Everything within the radius of the high chair tray was splattered with goop, including Kris. The only exception was his bib. It was spotless. "Even Harry Eastwood hasn't been shown the note although Matt did tell him about it when he and Sid broke the news to him about Bambi's death."

Calling for a time-out, JR whisked the baby upstairs for a cleanup and a mid-morning nap. While she was taking care of Kris and Mary was taking care of the last caramel roll, I ducked outside for a cigarette.

Reviewing the new information JR had managed to extract from Matt, I had the impression my police lieutenant son-in-law wasn't convinced that Bambi Eastwood's death had been a suicide. Unlike Hilly Murrow, who has never let the facts stand in the way of a good story, it also didn't sound to me that the fact-oriented Matt was ready to point the finger of guilt at Amanda Little, at least not this time.

JR returned to the kitchen, minus the freshly laundered Kris, who was sleeping off his breakfast. As was her habit, JR turned on the baby monitor. Stubbing out my nearly finished cigarette and depositing it in a nearby, sand-filled coffee can, I went back into the house.

"Maybe," said Mary as she cleared the table for JR out of consideration and her own good housekeeping habits, "Bambi was a victim of a crime of opportunity, you know like the elderly who get robbed when their Social Security checks come in or when some punk jumps out from behind a car in a downtown Indy parking garage and makes off with your purse."

"Mar, if that were the case, then her body would've been found in the garage or near the building's entrance rather than in the penthouse." I said, dismissing her theory on the grounds that it had no basis.

While I was mentally congratulating myself for rejecting what I considered to be an absolutely absurd theory, JR asked her favorite aunt whatever made her entertain such a possibility.

"Because there was no mention either in the newspaper or what Matt had to say that included one word or comment on Bambi's jewelry. My stars, everyone in Seville talked about how much jewelry she wore. And she wore it everywhere, even to the grocery store of all places!" Obviously, Mary believed that replenishing one's food supply was a no-frills chore.

"So what you're saying is that maybe the jewelry was the motive for Bambi's murder, if that's what it turns out to be. Matt didn't mention anything about jewelry or the place being ransacked but at this point, your theory is as good as any," said JR, adding that if she had the chance, she would ask Matt about the jewelry.

"Speaking of your husband, isn't that his unmarked car pulling into the driveway?" I announced, reaching for my purse, keys, and Mary. "Come on, Mar, we better get out of here before Lieutenant Kojak starts asking questions of his own, starting with what I've been up to lately. I always find it hard to fib when I'm within handcuff distance of the long arm of the law."

"I think what Mom's trying to say in her own unique way is that it's time for the two of you to vamoose," said JR, shooing her favorite aunt and me out the back door.

"Bye-bye, honey, I'll talk to you later," I said to my daughter, deliberately keeping my voice low as Mary and I scrambled down the back porch stairs. "Thanks for the info, your help, and the coffee. All three were appreciated."

"And don't forget to ask you-know-who about you-know-what. It'll be interesting to hear what Matt has to say about Bambi Eastwood's jewelry," bellowed Mary in a pitch loud enough to wake the dead and the napping Kris. "My stars, he certainly is a light sleeper."

Grabbing Mary by the arm, we made it to the van in

time to wave a good-bye to Matt and his trusty sidekick, Sergeant Sid Rosen, as they walked up the front porch stairs. Before visiting the Semple house, I had one more person I needed to interview—that is if Harry Eastwood was as warm and welcoming as I hoped he would be.

Chapter twenty-seven

❧

"I thought you said we were going to the Semple place," balked Mary as I turned the van onto a back road, "or was that another one of your little white lies?"

I lit a cigarette, rolled down the windows so that Mary wouldn't be subjected to the smoke, ignored the snipe at my truthfulness, and assured her that eventually the road would take us to the flip-project house.

"Okay, I believe you but is there some reason you had to pick this particular route? The road isn't even paved," Mary grumbled, fanning her lovely, dimpled face with her hands in a futile effort to rid the air of incoming road dust.

"Because this way is faster and also happens to pass right by Milt Cosgrove's old place." I said, expertly maneuvering the van around a flock of chickens that had wandered into the road from a nearby barnyard.

"So who cares? Milt doesn't even live there anymore. He and his wife, Ethel, bought matching Harley motorcycles when they both retired and took off for some biker rally in North or South Dakota. Herbie Waddlemeyer heard from Milt's cousin Floyd that the Cosgroves rented out their house, furniture and all, for megabucks."

"I don't know about the megabucks part," I said, slowing the van down as we approached an unmarked, one-lane bridge, "but I do know that the name on the rental agreement is Eastwood. And since we're in the neighborhood, I thought we should stop by and offer our sympathy to the bereaved Harry."

Ignoring Mary's request (actually it was more like a plea) that we skip the condolence call, I whipped the van up the long, steep drive that led to the house the Cosgroves still owned but no longer called home.

One of the prettiest ranch houses in the county, the long, low, and rambling redbrick building sits high on a grassy hill and is surrounded on three sides by a cluster of evergreen trees.

The white shutters that flank the tall windows across the front of the house match in style and color the simplicity of the covered porch's massive columns.

The red, oversized entrance door with its beveled-glass inserts and brass trim welcomes visitors as does the trio of gaily painted wooden rocking chairs placed at intervals along the porch deck.

Like the flagstone walk, the wishing well, the copper wind chimes, and the bird feeders, everything about the 1970s rambler issues an invitation to come and sit awhile.

"Oh jeez, I didn't expect to run into anyone besides the grieving husband," I said as I brought the van to a halt next to a late-model, expensive SUV that took up a large portion of the parking area next to the house.

Deliberately walking the long way around my own vehicle, I was able to get a good look at the SUV's license plate. The number on it indicated that it was from Hedley County, home to a number of fast-growing suburbs that sit within an easy drive to downtown Indianapolis.

"I wonder whose vehicle it is. With that number on the plate, at least we know it doesn't belong to the Castle Hills cops."

"You know what I wonder, Gin? I wonder what in the world we're doing here. I'd rather you tell me about that than where you think that big gas guzzler's from or who it belongs to," Mary groused. Climbing out of the van she struggled to stay upright as the spike heels of her black, patent-leather shoes began to slowly sink into the white gravel that covered the hillside parking area.

"Like I told you, we've come to offer our condolences to Harry Eastwood for the loss of his wife. It's the kind of thing that people from big cities expect people from small towns to do along with bringing platters of baked goods and easy-to-reheat casseroles made from a couple loaves of bread and a basket of fish." Seeing Mary's reaction (a mixture of disbelief and disgust), I admitted I was only kidding about the loaves and fishes.

Upon reaching the front door, Mary looked a bit worse for wear. With her black shoes covered in gravel dust and her white hair covered in road dust, Charlie's twin sister bore an uncanny resemblance to her brother when he is really, really upset with me. Rather than to bring this or her less-than-pristine appearance to her attention, I gave her a reassuring hug and rang the doorbell.

"Why, it's Mrs. Hastings. How nice of you to call at this awful time," exclaimed Harry Eastwood as he threw open the front door. Turning his attention to Mary he extended his hand. "Mrs. England. I believe that we've met at the country club or it might have been at that delightful Italian restaurant. Oh well, it really doesn't matter. It's nice to see you both again. Come in, ladies, come in."

Entering directly into what I would refer to as an informal living room/dining room combination, I immediately thought of the old TV show *The Brady Bunch*.

As did many homeowners in the 1960s and 1970s, the Cosgroves had allowed their own taste in decorating to be influenced by the entertainment industry. This is an industry that enjoys huge monetary gains by manipulating the public into believing what it sees is what it wants.

Those of us old enough to remember shag carpeting,

fiberglass draperies, black-and-gold mirror wall tiles, harvest gold appliances, avocado green telephones, swag lamps, and paneled walls more than likely selected our clothes in the same rote way that we selected our home decor.

In recent decades, individuality has resurfaced and choice has been returned to the person or persons who have to live with it. Perhaps if the Eastwoods had agreed to buy the house and furnishings instead of renting both, things would have been changed and updated. Or perhaps Bambi, a member of a much younger generation, believed the dated decor to be twenty-first-century retro.

Inviting us to make ourselves comfortable on the orange-and-avocado-green-upholstered, wedge-shaped, three-piece sectional sofa, Harry disappeared into the kitchen and returned with a most attractive, twenty-something young lady. The strong family resemblance between Harry and the girl made his explanatory introduction unnecessary.

"Mrs. Hastings, Mrs. England, I would like you to meet my daughter, Harriet Eastwood," he said, his face aglow with pride.

Once the formality was over, Harriet sat down on a nearby oversized, round, black-leather-covered ottoman. Crossing her long, designer jean–clad legs, she spoke openly about her father's second wife, Bambi, and the negative impact the marriage had on herself, her older brother Henry, and in particular, her mother, Helen.

"You ladies will probably think me horrid when I say this, but it's true. It's a relief not to have to deal with Bambi anymore. Once she wanted to do something, there was no stopping her. Like the time Bambi went over to the hospice, where she introduced herself to my grandmother as her new daughter-in-law, something that thoroughly confused Granny since my parents had decided not to tell her about their divorce and Daddy's remarriage."

Harriet paused and closed her dark eyes for a moment. I didn't know if the dark-eyed, dark-haired beauty was trying to remember the incident or forget it. When she opened her eyes, Harry made an attempt to change the subject but the determined girl was not about to let that happen.

Using her slender fingers to riffle her short hair into small swirls of waves, Harriet smiled at her father, and taking a deep breath, she continued. "The caregiver called my mother and we arrived in time to see Bambi being forcibly removed from the hospice. To say the air was blue from her language would be an understatement. My grandmother was so upset by then that she had to be sedated. Of course, Mother and I learned later that Daddy had done the unthinkable, as far as Bambi was concerned, which was to tell her what to do. In this instance, he'd told her to stay away from Granny so naturally, she went to see her. Would anyone care for a drink? I know I'm ready for one."

Easily unfolding her legs, Harriet Eastwood jumped to her feet and made her way over to the faux walnut bar with its Formica top and plentiful supply of glasses, ice, and liquor.

"I'll have a ginger ale," I said and without checking with her, I ordered Mary a diet cola. Harry was still nursing the cup of coffee he had in his hand when we arrived. I waited until Harriet had finished distributing the drinks to ask Harry, who had taken a seat at the bar, if he had made the mistake of telling Bambi what to do on Tuesday.

He was about to say something when his daughter butted in. "Let me answer that for you, Daddy," said Harriet, returning to the ottoman with a tumbler filled to the top with vodka and orange juice.

I wondered if Harriet's "take charge" personality was inherited from her mother or father or possibly from both. I hadn't a clue what had caused the Eastwood's divorce but if Harry and Helen had shared that type of personality, it could've put a real strain on their marriage.

"He made the mistake of telling Bambi not to drive to Indianapolis without him," said Harriet. "Naturally, she ignored my father's admonition. Bambi had what we psychiatrists consider a serious disorder. When someone, anyone,

gave her advice, she took it as a personal attack on her free
will. Being told what to do or not to do in Bambi's mind
was as unacceptable as it was unthinkable. In laymen's
terms, she was a borderline nutcase."

"Thank you, Dr. Eastwood." Harry beamed as he blew
her a kiss. "I couldn't have said it better myself. Bambi
called me on my cell phone late Tuesday afternoon to brag
about making the trip to Indianapolis without me. She said
that before driving back to Seville, she was going to shop
and help a friend with something. She didn't provide me
with any details."

"When she didn't come home, did you call the police?"
I could see that my question made Harry uncomfortable.

Clearing his throat, he hesitated but not long enough to
allow Harriet to jump in. "No, I didn't. I guess it doesn't
make any difference now that she's gone. You see, Bambi
has always been a free spirit and it wasn't the first time that
she, um . . . spent the night elsewhere."

"Come on, Daddy, admit it. Bambi was as loose as she
was dumb," declared Harriet, draining the contents of her
glass and slipping a partially melted ice cube in her mouth.
"She pawned the five-carat diamond wedding band you
gave her and spent the money on scads of costume jewelry.
She obviously thought more was better, be it jewelry or
men."

Directing her next comment to Mary and me, Harriet
added, "You should see the envelope stuffed with her
gaudy baubles that Lieutenant Cusak and Sergeant Rosen
dropped off here this morning. What she lacked in taste,
she made up in volume. That anyone would wear so much
jewelry, especially so many rings and on so many body
parts is unbelievable."

"You're right, of course." Harry sighed. "It's almost as
unbelievable as Bambi's suicide note. The girl was completely and hopelessly computer illiterate. Maybe I'm
clutching at straws but I think the person who murdered
Stuart Goodenough murdered Bambi and composed the
note."

"And did you mention any of this to anyone?" I asked, hoping that he expressed his opinion to Matt and not Hilly Murrow.

"I certainly did and that's about all I can say, at least for the present time. In fact I may have already said too much. Lieutenant Cusak warned me about loose lips sinking ships and the danger of getting mixed up with female amateur detectives. I think he was referring to that woman reporter from the *Seville Sentinel* although he didn't mention anyone by name."

Silently thanking God for small favors, I signaled to Mary that it was time to leave. When Harry walked us to the front door, I told him to expect a delivery from Billy Birdwell, whose mother, Sally Birdwell, is my next-door neighbor and owner of a B and B. Billy is Seville's best and newest caterer.

"I hope you and your charming daughter, Harriet, like finger food because Billy's making up a tray of spicy cheese wedges, buffalo wings, and everyone's favorite—freshly baked croissants stuffed with chicken salad. The food should be here in time for your dinner."

"Why, how very kind of you, Mrs. Hastings," said Harry, obviously pleased that small-town magnanimity was not a myth.

"You're quite welcome, but you should also thank Mrs. England. It's from both of us," I replied, taking Mary by the arm and steering her toward the van. In doing so, I prevented Harry from seeing the look of surprise on Mary's face. When he called out his "thank you" to the retreating Mary, she in turn called back her "you're welcome" to the hand-waving Harry.

While Mary was getting settled in the passenger seat, I buckled up, rolled the windows down, turned the key in the ignition, checked to see if perhaps the air conditioner had miraculously healed itself (it hadn't), and lit a cigarette. Releasing the parking brake and putting the van in reverse, I waited for Mary to buckle up, which she did but not before chastising me for fibbing.

"I'm surprised your tongue hasn't turned black from all the white lies coming out of your mouth lately. Telling that poor man to expect a delivery of food and from both of us at that. Honestly, Gin, you've hit a new low even for you."

"Why? Because I told the truth? By the way, Mar, you owe me for half the cost of the food plus tip plus delivery charge. Honesty may be the best policy, but it ain't cheap. You can pay me later. Now that we've gotten that settled, let's say we head for the Semple house, or would you rather I drop you off at home? Maybe this sleuthing business is too much for you."

Mary didn't bother using words to answer my question. The dark look she gave me spoke volumes.

Chapter
twenty-eight

A quick stop at Wally's Wienie Wagon for a couple of hot dogs with the works and two regular-size, lemon shake-ups and all was forgiven. I'd finished my dessert (a Tums) by the time we arrived at the Semple manse. What I found upon entering the house was enough to make me reach for another antacid tablet.

"Holy Moses, look what's happened to my beautiful, vanilla-colored, eggshell-finish walls and all the white trim JR spent hours painting. I haven't seen that much black on a light surface since great-uncle Fortesque Hastings fell into the fireplace when he was looking for his false teeth."

"Oh, I remember that." Mary giggled nervously. She was following so close behind me that were I to stop short we would've collided like two locomotives traveling on the same track. "You don't suppose he's returned from the dead and decided to take up residence in this old Victorian, do you?" Mary's voice was almost as shaky as her hand that was clutching the sleeve of my sweatshirt.

"Not unless he's come back as a crime scene investigator.

The black sooty-looking stuff is the powder used to find fingerprints and the powdery white stuff on the floors is used to find footprints, if I'm not mistaken. If anyone could come back from the grave to haunt the place, I'd say it would be Stuart Goodenough. What a shame. If he'd played it straight, everyone involved in the flip would have made a healthy profit and he'd probably be alive today."

"You think he was killed because he had sticky fingers?" Not waiting for an answer, Mary continued. "If that's the case, then shouldn't you be looking for evidence against Duke Demarco or Ben Kind or even that nice Harry Eastwood?"

Instead of answering the question, I lit a cigarette, ignoring the small, metal NO SMOKING sign I'd placed on the kitchen counter last Saturday in preparation for the open house. With cigarette in hand, I began a search of the cabinets.

Following my lead, Mary joined in the search. Huffing from all the bending and stretching, she stopped to catch her breath. "I haven't found anything yet but I think it would help if I knew what we were looking for," she said as her big blue eyes swept over the kitchen area.

"An ashtray or something that I can use for one, otherwise I'll have to flick the ashes in the sink."

The look that Mary gave me was as black as the powdery smudges on the sleeves of her blouse. "Some detective you are," she remarked, reaching behind me and snatching an avocado-colored beanbag ashtray from the windowsill above the sink. Because of its style and the fact that Bambi was a smoker, I assumed the ashtray came from the house that Harry was renting from the Cosgroves.

"Now that your unhealthy habit has been taken care of," growled Mary, "would you mind giving me some idea of what we are doing here other than tramping through sooty powder and smelling up the place with your stinky tobacco smoke?"

In addition to the smudges on her blouse, I noticed that

Mary also had a smudge of black on the tip of her nose. I would have brought it to her attention except that I had no desire to be the second dead body in the window seat. Moving on, I attempted to answer her question.

"Let's say that Vilma Beatty was right about seeing Stuart being dropped off at the house by Bambi. He must've had a good reason to enter the house, otherwise it would've made more sense for him to jump in his car, which was later found to be parked down the street, and hightail it back to the Castle Hills penthouse. Why stick around Seville any more than necessary when everyone connected with the flip was disgusted or angry with him? So whatever it was that made him go into the house had to be important."

"Like maybe he left his glasses or his car keys inside," suggested Mary. "If he was anything like my Denny or your Charlie, it probably was his keys. I never noticed if he wore glasses or not. I suppose it could have been glasses, but I think it was his keys."

"He wasn't like Denny or Charlie and he didn't come back to the house for keys or glasses!" I shouted in frustration.

Taking a deep breath, I got myself under control and, in a normal tone, continued my attempt to explain things to Mary. "Stuart's idea to rob Peter to pay Paul or in this case get money from Amanda Little to pay Duke Demarco fell apart when Amanda dumped him, forcing him to change plans. I think Stuart's coming back to the house was part of his new plan, which included meeting with the person he intended to con into giving him the money. For the con to work, the bait would have to be something the 'mark' wanted bad enough to pay for it. It would also have to be something that was accessible, which is why I believe it's somewhere in this house."

"Okay, let me get this straight," Mary said, resting her arms on the counter and unknowingly adding more smudges to her once-immaculate outfit. "On Saturday afternoon, Bambi drops Stuart off here at the house so he can meet with the 'mark' but something goes wrong and the 'mark' murders Stuart. Later, the 'mark' bumps off Bambi in Stuart's penthouse and tries to make it look like a suicide by leaving a fake note."

"By Jove, I think she got it," I said in my best light-hearted manner in an effort to make amends for my earlier Irish temper outburst.

"Well, not quite," admitted Mary. "Why bother looking for the bait here when the killer probably found it in the penthouse?"

"Because I don't think that's what happened. If I'm right about Stuart meeting with the 'mark' on Saturday for the purpose of getting money, remember what I said about the bait being accessible. It doesn't make sense to meet in Seville if the bait was stashed in Castle Hills. Like Judge Judy says, 'If it doesn't make sense, then it isn't true,' " I added, knowing that Mary, like myself, is an ardent fan of the former family court judge's television show. "I think Bambi and the 'mark' went to the penthouse looking for the bait. Again, something goes wrong and the 'mark' kills Bambi."

"My stars, Gin," Mary exclaimed, looking as excited as she sounded, "you've cracked another case."

It was my turn to say "not quite." "As to what went wrong and why Bambi was murdered, I think that's something only the killer can answer. I can't even tell you what Stuart used for bait even though I'm convinced that it's somewhere in this house. Once I know the what and the where, I intend to turn everything I've uncovered over to Matt and let him handle it."

"But, Gin," said Mary, sounding as worried as she looked, "Matt's liable to go ballistic about your meddling, I mean sleuthing."

"I guess I'll just have to take my chances and my lumps," I replied with more courage than I actually felt. Not wanting to dwell on the negative, I stubbed out my cigarette and stated in a positive voice that it was time to get down to business. "Come, Watson, we're about to match wits with the master of evil."

"I say, Holmes," replied Mary, slipping easily into the role of one of Arthur Conan Doyle's most beloved literary characters, "I hope we make it back to Baker Street in time for high tea."

"We will if you do as I say, my dear fellow, but we must stay alert and be wary," I said as I walked through the kitchen area and toward the door leading to the cellar. "Follow me as we go in search of the impossible dream."

"Wait a minute, Gin," cried Mary, reverting back to my childhood nickname and dropping the English accent, "isn't the impossible dream the name of a song from a Broadway musical?"

"Yeah but it was the best I could come up with. Keep your fingers crossed that we'll have better luck than Charlie did when he nosed around our cellar. He was crestfallen when I told him that the JFK note and signature on that old photo had nothing to do with the thirty-fifth president of the United States, John Fitzgerald Kennedy."

Chapter twenty-nine

Opening the cellar door, the darkness hit me along with the dank odor. "You wouldn't happen to have a flashlight on you, per chance?" I asked, not expecting Mary to have anything bigger than a tissue or a driver's license in her dinky purse. To my surprise, she produced a slim-line penlight that dangled from her equally slim-line wallet.

"Here, try this," she said, passing me the light along with the wallet, "it works but I can't guarantee for how long. The batteries are pretty old."

The penlight lasted just long enough for me to find the string that dangled from the single lightbulb fixture, the only source of electricity in the small, dirt-floor room. I returned the wallet and penlight to Mary and waited while she scooted back to the kitchen where she placed her purse next to mine on the island. She said she'd decided to follow my example of not being encumbered by anything in case we had to make a quick exit. I didn't bother to tell her that the reason my purse was on the island was not quite that complex—I had simply forgotten it.

"Come on, Mar," I called to her, "this lightbulb might

not last any longer than the one in the penlight. The last thing I want to do is stumble around in the dark." I shuddered, remembering the incident that occurred some two years earlier when I found myself in another dark and dank place. It was a creepy mausoleum and it took more than prayer and luck to get me out of that life-threatening situation.

With Mary by my side, we made a preliminary search of the room, finding nothing more than empty shelves thick with dust, some discarded picture frames, five in all, propped up in a corner, and a rusted kerosene lantern with a broken chimney discarded in a cardboard box along with a small, wadded-up piece of paper. Upon closer examination, the piece of paper appeared to be some sort of short list, but thanks to a combination of a soft lead pencil, crumpling, and age, the writing was practically illegible. I stuck the wrinkled paper in the pocket of my sweatpants and quickly moved on to a much more promising item of interest—a battered old trunk sitting in the middle of the malodorous cellar. The trunk was open and virtually empty except for what remained of a broken padlock. The lid of the trunk dangled precariously from one of the two hinges that was still attached to the back of the trunk. On closer examination, I was able to read the tattered, yellowed label that was in the process of detaching itself from the inside of the lid.

"Semple Seafaring Steamer Trunk Company, Seville, Indiana, 1894," I read aloud. "With a bit of restoration, I'll bet this old trunk would be worth a lot of dough. Maybe it ties into the reason Stuart came back to the house last Saturday. I saw one on the *Antiques Roadshow* a couple of weeks ago and the appraiser went gaga over it. I thought the guy who brought it to the show was going to go into cardiac arrest when he heard what it was worth." Expecting Mary to agree with me, she instead did as I did with Charlie and the JFK photograph and brought any dream of untold riches to a screeching halt. In Mary's opinion, other than sentimental value, the trunk was virtually worthless.

Because England's Fine Furniture also deals in antiques, I accepted what she had to say about the trunk but not without question. "But how come? The one on television looked a lot newer and a lot smaller and didn't even have a label. I thought in the world of antiques, provenance is everything."

"It sure is," Mary informed me, "and that's what makes the difference between this trunk and the one on TV. The guy had letters and photographs to back up his story about it being the trunk Amelia Earhart intended to take with her on what turned out be her last flight. Somehow, instead of being loaded on the plane, it was left behind in the hangar where it was virtually forgotten. Everyone assumed that the piece of luggage had disappeared, along with its owner, somewhere over the Pacific Ocean in 1937."

"Jeez, I must have missed that part when my cell phone went off. By the time I dug the thing out of my leather bag and told the caller that she had the wrong number, I made it back to the den just in time to hear the appraisal and see the guy's reaction."

The lightbulb began to flicker, something Mary took as a message from the long-departed Henry and Edna Mae Semple that it was time to leave the scene of their deaths and let their spirits rest in peace. I disagreed and took it as a message from Thomas Edison, the Wizard of Menlo Park, that it was time to change the lightbulb. With nothing more to see or examine in the room, Mary held the door open while I pulled the string, turned off the light, and made it out of the cellar in three giant steps. Even though I dismissed Mary's theory about what was causing the bulb to flicker, I wasn't taking any chances.

Once out of the cellar, Mary and I made an extensive tour of the house, checking on the condition of the borrowed furniture and accessories while we searched high and low for something, anything, that could've been the bait. In spite of our diligence, we came up empty. At the time I didn't realize that what we were looking for was hiding in plain sight.

"I think we're pretty well finished here," I said to Mary as we walked into the living room area. Plopping down on the little love seat that I'd shared with JR Saturday evening while we waited for someone to take our statement, I was struck by how much had changed yet stayed the same.

The fireplace with its marble mantel smudged in black looked almost as sad as the girl in the painting above it. Like a lot of the surfaces in the house, the portrait over the fireplace was in need of cleaning, but unlike the surfaces smudged with powdery residue, its dirty film was the result of coal dust, soot, tobacco smoke, and other indoor pollutants that had taken their toll on the painting over the years.

When I'd first come across the oil painting in the old, battered wardrobe cabinet, I'd been hesitant about using it due to its condition. I remember checking it over and discovering that someone, probably the artist, had attached a label to the back of the frame that named and dated the work of art. I hadn't been able to decipher the full name or date, although I was able to pick out certain letters such as two capital Es and what I took to be a small c along with a partial date of 19-something or other. The signature on the front left hand bottom corner of the portrait was partially obscured by the cheap frame and appeared to be either Gabe or Cabe. At the time, I secretly named it *A Study in Yellow*. I was snapped out of my reverie by the ringing of my cell phone. It was JR calling.

"Mom," she whispered into the phone, "don't talk, just listen. I'm in the pantry and Matt's upstairs changing his clothes. The autopsy on Bambi shows that like Loo's autopsy on Stuart Goodenough, there was GHB along with alcohol in her system. Only she had been given enough of the drug to kill her and it did. Oh, I almost forgot. It's now official—the penthouse had definitely been ransacked but what the killer was looking for, Matt didn't say and I didn't get a chance to ask. Listen, Mom, this whole thing is getting as complicated as it is dangerous. Please be careful." Having said all that, JR ended the call.

I'd already returned the phone to my purse when it rang again. It was Charlie calling to tell me that he was on his way home and to find out how my Chicago trip was going.

"Mary and I decided to spend the day right here in town. We spent the morning at JR's visiting with her and the baby. Then we went to the club for lunch and spent most of the afternoon looking at antiques. I'm really pooped and so is Mary. I suggest that you and Denny take us out to Farmer John's for the all-you-can-eat buffet. Tonight's special is roast beef and Yorkshire pudding." I was counting on Charlie's love of Yorkshire pudding (something his mother always made and I've never attempted) and Denny's tremendous appetite and love of a bargain to seal the deal.

As expected, Charlie and Denny took me up on my suggestion. When Charlie assured me that they'd be home within the hour, I in turn assured him that Mary and I would be ready and waiting.

"Okay, Mar," I said as I dropped the tiny phone into my overstuffed purse, "I think I better get us both home where we belong or we are going to have a lot of explaining to do, which might put dinner at Farmer John's or anywhere else in jeopardy."

"Gotcha," replied Mary before adding, "from what I've seen here, the CSI boys have a lock on things and other than checkin' on the goods from the store, our trip here was a bummer. I say we hit it."

Oh dear God, I said to myself, what in the world have I done? First JR's clandestine phone calls and now Mary's tough talk. I've turned my lovely daughter and her favorite aunt into Starsky and Hutch! Maybe this time I really should stick to decorating and keep my nose out of Matt's business. But as in the past, it was a thought and only a thought. I was in too deep to back out now. To me it would be equivalent to leaving a design project half finished or putting a book away without reading the final chapter. I knew that I wouldn't or couldn't do either one of those things any more than I could or would walk away from solving the puzzle of what was now a double murder.

Less than an hour later, I was back at Kettle Cottage, showered, dressed, and waiting to be wined and dined. As I sat back and enjoyed a cup of reheated coffee and a cigarette, I thought about the day, beginning with the visit to JR's and ending with the visit to the flip-project house. Although I didn't agree with how Mary phrased it, I did agree that the visit to the old Victorian was not exactly a smashing success insofar as learning anything new or helpful for my flagging investigation.

Antsy from a combination of frustration, hunger, and waiting for Charlie to arrive home, I left my cup of coffee and the napping Pesty (she was enjoying her usual in-between-meal snooze) and dashed up the oak staircase and into the master bed and bath. Scooping up the black sweat suit I'd worn all day and the dark blue towels I'd used when I took my shower, I carried them down the stairs and into the laundry nook where I tossed the small load into the washer.

The water had almost covered the soiled towels and the sweat suit when it dawned on me that I'd forgotten to check the pockets of my sweatpants. It wouldn't be the first time that I threw in a load of laundry that came out looking as though it had been caught in a storm of confetti thanks to a forgotten grocery receipt or worse yet, a tissue.

Plunging my hand into the washer, I snagged the sweatpants on the first try and fished out a soggy, wadded-up piece of paper. It was the piece of paper that I'd found in the cardboard box in the Semple house cellar. With as much care as I could muster, I opened the soggy paper and gently smoothed it out as best I could and left it to dry on top of the old but dependable Maytag dryer. Maybe by morning, I reasoned, the paper would be dried out enough to be handled. If its message could be deciphered was another story and one that only time would tell.

"Hey, sweetheart, your lover boy is home," Charlie called out, attempting to determine what room I was in and at the same time trying for a laugh.

"Okay, lover boy," I answered with a loud, faux giggle,

"come to the laundry nook and if you hurry, maybe you'll get lucky before my husband gets home."

After a warm but proper greeting (a nice kiss and hug) Charlie disappeared into the master bath for a quick shower and change of clothes while I watched the end of the network news. The news was followed by *Jeopardy*! Settling back in Charlie's well-worn reclining chair, I tried to match wits with the three contestants, all former five-time winners. By the time Alex gave the three contestants the reminder to be sure that the final answer is in the form of a question, Charlie came into the den looking spiffy and, according to him, starving to death.

"If that's true, Charlie, do me a favor and die quietly. I've watched this entire program waiting for you to get ready and I'd like to hear the final answer and question."

"No problem," he said pleasantly as he left the room. "I'll be waiting for you in the kitchen."

The category was the Great Depression, a subject that had always fascinated me since I had a mother and a father who grew up in that era of truly hard times and talked about it almost constantly. I had missed most of the answers in the categories of nuclear chemistry, astronomy, sixteenth-century poets, Mayan mythology, and astrophysics but now here was a category that I actually knew something about, thanks to my parents. I listened closely as Alex read the final answer, "An artist of great promise whose work has recently . . ."

"Hey, Jean," shouted Charlie from the kitchen and effectively drowning out Alex's honey-toned voice, "are the car keys in there?"

"No, I don't see them," I answered. Without the aid of my reading glasses (I'd misplaced them again) I'd accidentally hit the volume button on the TV's remote control instead of the mute button.

"What did you say?" shouted Charlie all the louder. "I can't hear you with the television blasting." Striding into the den, Charlie picked up the remote, turned down the volume so low that I doubt if even a pod of dolphins could pick up what was being broadcast, and proclaimed, "I must have left them on the dresser in the bedroom. Sorry, sweetheart."

Before heading upstairs in search of the keys, Charlie handed me the remote control along with the suggestion that I have Doc Parker check my hearing. "You had the TV so loud sweetheart, I'm surprised your eardrums didn't break."

Thanks to Charlie's misplaced keys and my misplaced glasses, I'd missed the audio portion of the final minutes of the show and caught only a fleeting glimpse of the winner's written answer: Who was Gabe? Or had she scribbled: Who was Cabe?

"Jean," Charlie called out, "you ready to go?" Not waiting for a reply, he announced that he would be waiting for me in the car.

I turned off the television, picked up the car keys from the kitchen table where he'd left them, and caught up with Charlie before he died of starvation.

On the drive to Farmer John's where we were meeting Mary and Denny for dinner, my Irish intuition was telling me that one way or another I needed to find out more about the artist whose name was Cabe, or was it Gabe? I promised myself that I would do that ASAP even if it killed me.

Chapter
thirty

﹆

Friday morning was a virtual repeat of Thursday with plenty of blue skies, sunshine, warm temperatures, and moderate humidity, all of which lived up to the local forecast of yet one more summer day despite the lateness of the season. While the East and West Coasts can brag about their oceans, the South about its hospitality, and the North about its rugged terrain, the Midwest can brag about its tenacity in following the seasons of the year as designated by the calendar.

Midwesterners take warm summers, cool autumns, freezing winters, and rain-soaked springs as a given and rarely experience radical changes in the weather that the aforementioned regions of the country have had to deal with on more than one occasion. While some learned souls blame such occasions on global warming, people in the Midwest blame it on geographical location.

I knew without having to ask that just as a certain ball of fur never misses a meal, my husband and his brother-in-law never miss an opportunity to golf eighteen holes at Sleepy Hollow's course when the weather and the sprinklers are in sync. A quick look out the open half of the Dutch door, followed by a quick call to the club's pro shop, and Charlie was ecstatic with both the weather and the news that the greens and fairways were back to being in tip-top condition.

"Do me a favor, will you, sweetheart," said Charlie as he reached for the phone to share the good news with Denny, "drop the box of golf magazines in the garage off at the library. I promised Mrs. Milhower I'd have it there in time for the book fair. If I remember right, it's scheduled for today."

I was about to inform him that the fair was scheduled for Saturday, not Friday when it occurred to me that with Mrs. Milhower's reputation as a computer whiz who loves a good challenge, she might like to take a crack at my Gabe/ Cabe quandary. I needed to know more about the artist before leaping to any conclusions as to the *A Study in Yellow* painting's worth as Charlie had with the JFK photo and I did with the Semple steamer truck before being set straight.

"Sure, no problem, chum. You're in luck. I was headed for the library anyway," I said with more enthusiasm than I generally exhibit before nine o'clock in the morning, causing Charlie's eyebrows to register his surprise by climbing halfway up his forehead. He was about to question my unusual sunny, early morning disposition but just then Denny came on the line, shifting Charlie's attention away from me and redirecting it to his own quandary—whose turn was it to drive? His or Denny's?

Leaving Charlie on his own to solve the problem, I took my coffee, cinnamon toast, and cigarettes and went out on the patio to enjoy my little corner of the great outdoors. As was her choice, Pesty remained in the great indoors. I'd learned a long time ago that Keeshonds prefer to make up their own minds on what to do or not to do. If Pesty had wanted to come outside, there would have been no stopping her, and if she didn't, there was nothing or nobody that could change her mind short of the house burning down or outright bribery.

Enjoying the comfort of a cushioned wicker chair and with the solutions to my immediate corporeal needs (nourishment, caffeine, and nicotine) set within arm's reach atop a small, wicker table, I used logic to review what puzzle pieces I'd managed to collect in my investigation: Amanda's story of betrayal; Horatio's report on Stuart and Bambi; Ben Kind and Duke Demarco's shared alibi for Stuart's murder; the role played by GHB in the two murders; the ransacking of the Castle Hills condo; information gleaned from my interviews with Arthur Kraft, Harry Eastwood, Vilma Beatty, and Biddy McFarland; plus all the official inside info that JR managed to pass on to me unbeknownst to my police lieutenant son-in-law.

I had a hunch that with the exception of two or possibly three pieces, I already had enough of the puzzle to make an educated guess regarding the who and how of the two murders, but I was baffled as to the what and the why. If the luck of the Irish stayed with me, then my trip to the library would provide information that could change my guess to a provable fact.

"A penny for your thoughts," Charlie whispered in my ear. He had taken me completely by surprise, causing me to slosh coffee on my new, beige walking shorts and expensive, matching V-neck sweater.

"Forget the penny, chum. I'd rather have some cold water to get the coffee stains out before they set. As for what I'm thinking right now, trust me—you don't want to know."

My husband's apology for taking me by surprise was followed by the sound of Denny's ancient MG pulling into the driveway. Placing the once-full cup of coffee on the little table, I braced myself for the usual good-bye kiss and hug. What I received instead was a pat on the head followed by Charlie's explanation.

"I decided not to push my luck," he said. "First, I stick you with the job of lugging the box of magazines to the library, then because of me, you spilled coffee all over your outfit. By the way, it looks good on you in spite of the spots.

The way things are going, who knows what might happen if I tried to give you a kiss. Consider the pat on the head as damage control."

"Hey, don't worry about it. I'm pretty sure I can get the spots out and as far as sticking me with going to the library, like I said when you asked me, I'm headed there anyway," I replied, flashing a smile. "And to show you that you're forgiven, I'll make your favorite dinner tonight. Double cheeseburgers with homemade French fries, coleslaw, and barbecued beans."

"Double cheeseburgers!" exclaimed Charlie, practically drooling at the menu I'd rattled off. "Are you kidding me?"

For a moment there, I almost confessed that I'd already answered the age old question of what's for dinner while brushing my teeth and the menu was based on availability and not on forgiveness but I didn't. My mama didn't raise a fool. Besides, the ground beef had already been defrosted.

Our lighthearted conversation was interrupted by a series of toots from the MG's horn, something that most likely rousted out of bed any late-sleeping guests at our neighbor Sally Birdwell's B and B.

"Hey, kid, I better get going before Denny either wears out his hand or the horn," said Charlie as he headed for the driveway. "See you later, probably around three. Four at the latest."

"That works for me. I should be home myself by then. Have fun and don't forget to duck," I teased, alluding to an incident from the not-too-distant past when Charlie's knee was broken by a golf ball courtesy of Denny's errant tee shot.

"Need I remind you that your own track record of avoiding mishaps hasn't been all that great," said Charlie, his smile matching the twinkle in his steely blue eyes. "Maybe you should consider spending the whole day at the library. At least then you'll be out of harm's way."

I realized that Charlie's harm's way remark was meant to be a joke and not a foreshadow of what fate might have in store for me but nonetheless I felt a sudden chill that sent me scurrying back to the safety of Kettle Cottage.

My efforts to expunge the coffee spots from the beige shorts and sweater using tap water and a paper towel were less than satisfactory. I found the prospect of ending up with yet another outfit resplendent with permanent spatters of Juan Valdez's favorite brew to be depressing.

Stripping off the sweater and walking shorts in the privacy of the bathroom, I slipped into my less-than-flattering but clean and ready-to-wear, green chenille jumpsuit and hurried down the oak staircase to the laundry nook. Setting the Maytag on low, cold, gentle cycle and crossing my fingers for luck, I tossed the new outfit into the washer along with measured amounts of detergent and non-chlorine bleach.

Remembering the towels and black sweats that I'd left to dry the night before, I emptied the dryer and used the top of it as a temporary parking place for the small stack of clean laundry. I was about to return to the kitchen when something on the floor of the alcove caught my eye. It was the little wrinkled piece of paper.

"Oh wow," I exclaimed as I addressed the list as though it was a living thing, "I almost forgot about you. I don't know why but for some reason someone, probably Edith, thought you were important enough to save and put you in that box in the cellar. Now it's time to share your secret with me." Picking up the paper, I rushed out of the alcove and into the kitchen where the light was better only to discover that I needed more help than reading glasses and bright sunshine.

A frantic search of my kitchen desk was followed by an equally frantic search of the cabinet junk drawer where I unearthed everything from my voter registration card to an assortment of nails, expired coupons, Band-Aids, old nail polish, and tangled extension cords. Everything that is, except the one item I needed, which was a magnifying glass.

Frustrated, I struck a pose reminiscent of Charlton Heston when, as Moses in *The Ten Commandments*, he commanded the Red Sea to part. "Magnifying glass, I order you to appear in my kitchen," I bellowed dramatically, sounding more like Bugs Bunny on steroids than the leader of the Israelites.

Needless to say, my behavior aroused the curiosity of Pesty, who stared at me with her round, dark chocolaty eyes before disappearing into the den. Returning a few moments later, she deposited the magnifying glass at my feet. For a moment, I was stunned and almost speechless.

"One of these days, girlfriend," I informed the self-assured little Kees as she sauntered back to her favorite spot under the kitchen table to resume her nap, "you're going to have to tell me how you did that."

With magnifying glass in hand, I sat down at the table and studied the faded, crumpled paper. From what I could tell, which wasn't very much, it was a list of some sort. A study of the slant and continuity of the surviving alphabetic characters led me to conclude that the author of the list had been schooled in the old Palmer method of writing, which reinforced my belief that Edith and the author were one in the same.

Tearing off a fresh piece of paper from a dog-eared notepad that I'd come across during my futile search of the junk drawer, I attempted, using a pencil, to duplicate the few, barely legible alphabetic characters that managed to survive. The longer I labored, the more it continued to be a puzzling mystery to me.

When I was satisfied that I had given it my best shot, I sat back and studied what I compiled:

```
Lo   i  Li
Ra  ia  t in R  d
B  aut  in B   k
G   iou  G a
Pos d    P  ple
Eth r l in    cru
```

"Terrific," I remarked aloud despite the fact that other than the sleeping Pesty, I was alone in the house, "another puzzle in need of solving. Now that's something I don't need."

Checking the clock, I was aghast to see how much time I'd spent working on the list. I had to get to the library and Mrs. Milhower before she departed for home and her midday meal. I was well aware that, according to the town gossips, the prim and proper head librarian has been known to indulge in a post-lunch nip and nap, returning to the library after story hour. Having experienced the joys of story hour firsthand as a volunteer, I didn't blame her for tossing back an occasional shot of schnapps. Because I needed Mrs. Milhower's help more than she needed an extended lunch break, I dropped everything, threw my copy of the list in my purse, grabbed the keys to the van, and made it to the library in record time.

Chapter
thirty-one

✌

"You say you don't know anything about the artist other than the name of Cabe or possibily Gabe? Oh my, you certainly haven't given me much to go on," said the tall and stately Mable Milhower, peering down at me through the pince-nez perched on the bridge of her long, aristocratic nose. "This may take a while but let me see what I can do. You're not in a hurry, are you?"

In addition to being the head librarian and a whiz on the computer, Mable Milhower is also the most intimidating person in all of Seville, which is why I answered in the negative. Leaving Mrs. Milhower to do her thing, I found an empty table in a quiet corner of the reference room where I thought I would pass the time working on my copy of the puzzling list.

Two hours later, I was no closer to a solution than I was when I worked on it in my kitchen, but I did have a nice, long nap. A quick trip to the LADY'S LAVATORY (I kid you not—that's the wording selected by the library board and subsequently painted on the door in gold letters) to splash cold water on my face and I was ready to check on Mrs. Milhower's progress.

Stepping up to the main desk, my heart sank. There was no sign of Mrs. Milhower and the hands on the big wall clock were pointing to twelve. To make matters worse, it was story hour day. If the town gossips were right, then the head librarian was taking an extended lunch hour and I had no intention of spending the entire day in the library, regardless of Charlie's joking suggestion.

I was about to cut my losses and leave when a freckle-faced young man with ginger-colored hair and bright green eyes came bustling over to where I was standing. There was something vaguely familiar about him and I was about to find out what that something was.

"Hi there," he said in a most pleasant voice, "you must be Mrs. H. Mrs. M. went home for lunch but she left this for you," he said handing me a large envelope that Mrs. Milhower, the soul of discretion, had marked with my name and sealed with tape.

The library employee name tag had been pinned upside down on the breast pocket of the young man's white, short-sleeve dress shirt, making it a bit difficult to make sense out of his name. At first glance it appeared to be for-eign but upside down or not it soon became as plain as the freckles on his face and his use of alphabet speak that the young man was Tammie Flower's (the hostess with the most-est) younger brother Tommy.

I gave Tommy a five-dollar bill along with my instruc-tions for him to give it, along with my thanks, to Mrs. Milhower when she returned.

"If she finds that it isn't enough," I said over the din of squealing voices coming from the story hour reading area, "tell her to bill me. If it goes the other way and she finds that I overpaid, tell her I said to donate it to the story hour fund. If I remember right from my own days as a volunteer reader, the story hour is always in need of money to replen-ish the program's first-aid kit."

"Got it, Mrs. H. And don't you worry none. All us

Flowers have a knack for remembering things, especially names and stuff like complicated messages."

In an effort that I could only suppose was an attempt by Tommy to prove this, he repeated my message of thanks and instructions about the money. Since nothing other than proper names were lost in the young man's unique rendering of what I'd said, clutching the envelope from Mrs. Milhower, I bid adieu to Mrs. F.'s son and headed for the nearest exit, my van, and the peace and quiet of Kettle Cottage.

Passing within eardrum-breaking distance of the story hour's overly enthusiastic group of preschoolers, I paused long enough to catch the program's latest volunteer reader making a valiant attempt to keep her audience's attention on the book she was reading by showing the book's pictures and asking questions.

"See children, this is Ralphie with his new tricycle. Who can tell me what his mother told him about riding it in the street? What did she say could happen?"

A chorus of screams went up along with a show of hands. A chubby little girl with plenty of lung power shouted out that Ralphie's mommy said to stay out of the street and away from danger. The rest of the children picked up on this answer and soon were shouting in agreement.

Too bad Bambi never read the story of Ralphie and the tricycle, I thought to myself as I walked out of the library and over to where I'd parked the van. But as Dr. Harriet Eastwood pointed out, I reminded myself as I climbed in the van and lit a cigarette, Bambi had a serious problem with being told what to do.

My return to Kettle Cottage was without fanfare. Pesty, believing that she'd been gypped out of a midday snack, was sulking in front of the pantry cabinet door and only acknowledged my presence by whining her displeasure. Her demeanor changed for the better when I shared my late lunch of cream cheese, peach preserves, and soda crackers with the spoiled pooch. Normally, I would not have done so but after her Lassie-like response to my magnifying glass dilemma, I felt I owed the little Kees something better than a rock-hard Dandy Diet doggy treat.

Once our creature comfort needs had been sufficiently satisfied, I cleared the table, located my misplaced reading glasses (they were in my purse and the last place I looked), and sat down to read the fruits of Mrs. Milhower's technological labors. If I hadn't been wearing my glasses, I wouldn't have believed my eyes.

Chapter thirty-two

Thanks to the information the head librarian managed to gather despite the little I'd given her to work with, I learned a bit about the world of art and a gifted artist by the name of Cabe, not Gabe. The following was taken from Mrs. Milhower's computer findings:

According to his bio, Cabe was born in Boston on St. Valentine's Day either in 1907 or possibly 1908. The exact year cannot be verified due to the fact that his parents were part of the flood of European immigrants who because of social, economic, and language barriers often let others take care of filling out documents for them. This led to mistakes being made, some innocently and some deliberately. Not much is known about Cabe's early years other than by the time he reached the age of sixteen, both his parents had died. A distant relative in Chicago took him in and for the next few years Cabe studied off and on at the Art Insitute under the watchful eye of Paulina Racine, a local artist and teacher of some renown. During the Great Depression, he signed on with the Works Progress Administration, a federal agency created by President Franklin D. Roosevelt. When he wasn't painting murals on government buildings or designing posters for government agencies, Cabe did what he did best, which was to paint beautiful portraits of beautiful women. The artist signed his name using a combination of his first and last names. Calvin Bean thus became Cabe. The half dozen portraits that he'd completed before his death in 1935 are known in art circles as the Six Sisters. In the mid-1950s, the portrait Lovely in Lilac *was the first of the six paintings to surface. Subsequently, in the decades that followed, four others have also mysteriously surfaced, each portrait selling for more than its predecessor. Reliable sources report that fifth in the Six Sisters series,* Posed in Purple, *sold for a cool quarter of a million dollars, leading the experts to speculate that the sixth and last painting, if and when it surfaces, will sell for more than the combined amount realized from the sale of the previous five.*

The report ended with the suggestion to contact the Library of Congress, Chicago's Art Institute, and Sotheby's for further information and/or updates on the artist's work.

When I finished digesting the information, I decided to have another shot at filling in the blanks on Edith's list. I was pleasantly surprised how easy it was once I knew what I was looking for:

Lovely in Lilac
Radiant in Red
Beauty in Black
Gracious in Gray
Posed in Purple
Ethereal in Ecru

Lighting a cigarette, I sat back and enjoyed the "eureka!" moment and thought about what Vilma Beatty had said about Calvin's wedding gift to Edith. "I'd bet my life that the gift and *Ethereal in Ecru* are one in the same," I said to the disinterested Pesty. I didn't bother to inform my furry friend that Calvin Bean died on the eve of the wedding, leaving Edith with a broken heart along with the Six Sisters series, which increased in value over the years. I was also willing to bet that Edith was responsible for selling off the portraits over the years. It most likely was how she supported herself and enabled her to reject the fortune left to her by her parents. The five empty frames I found in the cellar confirmed this, at least it did for me.

If my hunch was right, I knew where to find the last of the Six Sisters series. Now all I had to do was gather up a few loose ends and turn everything I had on the case over to my son-in-law, Matt. Unlike in the past, this time I didn't feel as though my amateur sleuthing had interfered with the official investigation, nor had I placed myself or others, particularly JR or Mary, in a position of needing to be rescued in the nick of time by Matt and Co. While my evidence for the most part was circumstantial, I figured that when it was combined with the physical evidence uncovered by the police, whoever ended up prosecuting the case would be elated.

In my mind's eye, I pictured myself on the witness stand testifying against the murderer. Dressed smartly in a designer suit and with my hair and makeup picture perfect, à la Joan Crawford (minus the shoulder pads and big eyebrows), I would stand up and point a perfectly manicured finger at the accused and say in a clear, crisp, voice: "There is the person who because of greed ended the lives of two not-so-innocent people." Maybe my remark about the victims would be considered by some to be a bit harsh but I'm under oath to tell the truth and when it really counts, I never lie.

I was brought back to reality by the sound of the grandfather clock in the front hall striking the hour. It was one o'clock, leaving me only two hours for loose-end gathering. I needed to be back home in time to make Charlie his double cheeseburger dinner. Thanking the gods for frozen French fries, deli coleslaw, canned barbecued beans, and a husband that doesn't know the difference between home-made and store bought, I gave Pesty instructions not to answer the phone. In view of the magnifying-glass epi-sode, I wasn't taking any chances, but since she was nap-ping at the time, I don't think my message got through.

With a nod to the happiest mouse telephone that be-longed in the happiest place on earth and not in my kitchen, I closed and locked both the top and bottom of the Dutch door. Once outside, I climbed into my van and headed for a fast visit with Vilma Beatty.

Chapter thirty-three

✺

Remembering the hissy fit Biddy had last time because I hadn't called ahead, I decided to call her on my cell phone. Pulling into a parking spot in Finklestein's Pharmacy's lot, I made the call without endangering myself or others. I call it being careful. Charlie calls it being smart and JR, who narrowly avoided being struck by a driver who ran a four-way stop sign while using a cell phone, calls it using your car as a car and not a motorized telephone booth.

"The McFarland residence, Bridget McFarland speaking," said the familiar voice using her less-familiar given name. "Who's calling, please?"

"Biddy, it's me, Jean Hastings. I was wondering if it would be okay with you and your mother, if I stopped by in a few minutes. There's a little something I need help with and I think that possibly your mom can help me. It has to do with memory recall." I felt that this was a nice way of putting it without resorting to the absolute truth or an outright lie.

"Oh my, it's Charlie, isn't it? When Gordy ran into him at the gas station, I believe it was early on Thursday morning, my hubby asked your hubby how you were doing and your hubby said that you were off to Chicago with Mary England. Everyone in town knows that you and Mary England were out at the old Cosgrove place paying your respects to that poor unfortunate man, Mr. Eastwood. Has he been doing that a lot lately?" Biddy inquired with more sympathy in her voice than a convention of funeral directors. "You know, mixing up names of people with places like Chicago with Cosgrove."

"Who? Mr. Eastwood or Charlie?" I asked, tongue in cheek and not surprised that the queen bee of gossip knew of my visit to the old Cosgrove ranch house.

"Charlie of course," huffed Biddy. Before I could confirm or deny what she was insinuating, Biddy gave me the opening I'd hoped for yet never dreamed would be so easy to get.

"Jean, dear, as long as you're coming over to visit with Mother, do you think you could possibly stay awhile? The ladies in my bridge club are planning on dropping in on poor Mr. Eastwood and bringing him some casseroles and covered dishes. I would love to go if only I had someone to keep Mother company in my absence. I won't be long, I promise you. Normally, Gordy would be only too happy to sit with Mother but one of the freezers at the ice cream store suddenly went on the fritz. In Gordy's line of work, one has to be able to respond to any disaster regardless of the day or hour."

"Yeah, just like FEMA," I said sardonically, something Biddy either didn't notice or chose not to notice. I had a hunch that it was the latter rather than the former. Like most gossips, Biddy is apolitical.

"Listen, Biddy, if it'll help you out, I'll be more than happy to keep your mother company. Just don't be gone too long. I promised Charlie I'd be home in time to fix his favorite dinner and you know yourself how long it takes to cook from scratch." I added the last part for the hell of it and to see how much time it would take for the word to get around town that I was a gourmet cook.

Biddy and I agreed on a time, giving me ten minutes to kill before I turned up at her door. I used the time to smoke a cigarette in the privacy of the van and to thank St. Patrick for extending my luck to include a visit with Vilma sans Biddy.

Although Vilma Beatty used a scooter to get around because age had taken a toll on her legs, making walking difficult, there was nothing wrong with the rest of her, including her mind and her eyesight that I'd observed despite what Biddy claimed. In my opinion, Vilma Beatty wasn't ready to sit in the background like an antique to be admired but not used. No, I said to myself, remembering the wink the old lady gave me after she'd administered the tongue lashing to Biddy, I'd rather have Vilma in my corner than Biddy, who's been known to panic watching a scary movie.

When we were kids, Biddy crawled under the seats in the balcony of the now-defunct Odeum Theater during the showing of *Abbott and Costello Meet Frankenstein*. It took two ushers and the manager, Mr. Waddlemeyer, Herbie's father, to pull the terrified girl out from where she was hiding and escort her out of the theater and onto the sunlit sidewalk.

Pushing the memory of an adolescent Biddy covered head to toe in popcorn residue, melted malt balls, and partially chewed jujubes back into a special niche in my mind, I brushed on some lip gloss, fluffed up my hair, and headed for the grown-up Biddy's house.

As I brought the van to a halt at the curb in front of the McFarland's beautifully restored painted lady, I wondered if the gossip maven remembered that it was me who dumped the last of my popcorn on her head and then dutifully reported Biddy's screaming theatrics to the management. Thanks to my snitching on her, Biddy was banned from the place. When Hitchcock's *Psycho* was showing there, even though it was years later, old man Waddlemeyer refused to sell her a ticket.

From the enthusiastic greeting I received when Biddy

opened the front door and invited me inside, I assumed that my volunteering to stay with Vilma so that Biddy could lead the charge of the gossip brigade on Harry Eastwood had cancelled out the sins of my youth.

"Thank you so much, Jean, for keeping Mother company. Normally, I only leave her on Wednesday, as you well know, and for only an hour or so at the very most but, I do think that we need to support poor Harold, who must be grieving at the sudden loss of his dear wife, Bunny," gushed Biddy, looking almost as distressed as she did when she was bounced out of the Odeum Theater a jillion Saturday matinees ago.

"You're welcome, Biddy. I enjoy your mother's company. By the way, it's Harry, not Harold, and Bambi, not Bunny," I said, stepping into the entrance hall with its sweeping stairway, mile-high ceiling, and carved crown molding.

"Harry who?" Biddy demanded to know, apparently forgetting for a moment that, as far as she knew, she needed me more than I needed her.

"Harry Eastwood, the grieving husband of dear Bambi Eastwood, who had the bad fortune to die much sooner than either poor Harry or Bambi herself ever expected."

"Oh yes, you're quite right, Jean, I mean about the names of course. You'll have to pardon me. The thought that my little group can bring comfort, even if it's only food and kind words, is so paramount in my mind that minor details such as inconsequential nicknames aren't all that important."

I was about to inform her that Harry might beg to differ with her on the whole name thing but the sound of a beeping horn brought an end to that conversation.

"That's my ride. I must go," trilled Biddy, her face glowing with excitement. She reminded me of a hunter going in for the kill. "The tea cart is ready and waiting for you in the elevator. So is Mother. I mean she's on her scooter. Not on the elevator. Upstairs. Oh bother, you know what I'm trying to say."

Patting her perfectly coiffed hairdo, she checked her reflection in the dark oak–framed mirror in the entrance hall. Obviously pleased, Biddy proceeded to gracefully float out the door without so much as a "hello, good-bye, stick your nose in cherry pie," which was an expression my late father often used and never explained, but I think you get the idea. Biddy was not about to waste any more of her precious time on me. She had a bigger fish to fry.

Chapter thirty-four

True to her word, Biddy had the tea cart ready and waiting when I stepped into the elevator for the short trip to Vilma Beatty's sitting room, part of the suite that Designer Jeans had planned and executed for the gracious elderly woman. Despite inviting Biddy and Gordon to make themselves at home when she moved out of the old Victorian following the death of her husband, Vilma (knowingly or not) projected an aura that left no doubt in a visitor's mind who was the real mistress of the manor—Vilma Hale Beatty, a retired navy nurse who was stationed in the South Pacific during the Second World War.

Coming from a military family and in view of her own time in the service, it was almost inevitable that Vilma would meet, fall in love, and marry a military man. In 1945, destiny took its course and Vilma married Captain T. R. Beatty, son of Major Sherman Beatty, a veteran of the Spanish-American War. Captain Beatty, who served in both World War II and the Korean War, was a decorated war hero as was his father, the major.

Vilma filled me in on all of this while we made short

work of the lavish tea that Biddy had prepared for us. Vilma, despite looking as frail as a piece of porcelain, polished off most of Biddy's buttery pound cake, a half dozen creamy bonbons, and a pitcher of sweet tea. I pretty much stuck to black coffee and one cherry-filled tart.

Making sure that Vilma had had enough of everything, I loaded up the cart with what little remained of the goodies, along with the napkins, plates, cups, and silverware. Pushing it into the elevator, the tea cart and I made the quick trip to the first floor, where I left the cart in the back hall before hurrying back to the elevator and the waiting Vilma.

Once back in Vilma's second-floor sitting room, I pushed a comfortable club chair closer to the settee that Vilma had moved to during my short absence, leaving her scooter parked under the long, double window that faced the side yard of the flip property. I was contemplating how to bring up the subject of the color of the dress Edith wore for her wedding present portrait when Vilma coughed. It was more of an ahem rather than a sharp hack, but it got my attention.

"What in the name of all that's holy are you thinking about, Jean? You look as though you've got something serious on your mind. Why don't we talk about it. Maybe it'll help."

For the first time in a very long time, I missed my mother and wondered if, like Vilma, she would someday choose to spend her sunset years in an upstairs sitting room tastefully done in a plethora of basically newly acquired things from the rug on the floor to the pictures on the walls, courtesy of Designer Jeans's magnificent design plan. That's when it hit me. I should have incorporated more of Vilma Hale Beatty into the plan and less interior design correctness.

Like everyone else, I'd been completely taken in by her gentile manner and frail physical appearance. The bulky, twin-handled knitting bag always within easy reach of her favorite chair also did nothing to dispel Vilma's image of someone whose experiences in life never involved anything beyond hearth and home.

"Jean, dear, if you'd rather not discuss it with me, I understand. I didn't mean to pry. Believe me, I may be old but I'm not nosy, and unlike my daughter, I do mind my own business."

"Oh, Mrs. Beatty, please forgive me," I said, realizing that she took my lapse into silence as a rejection of her invitation to speak my mind. "I was trying to figure out how to ask you about the color of Edith's wedding finery. I assume it was white, right?"

"Wrong. Unlike the young girls of today, back then white wasn't the must-wear color for a wedding. Edith's dress was a grayish yellow. I believe it's called ecru. If I close my eyes, I can see her standing there in the yard looking like an angel. That image of her is the first thing I thought of when I saw that young man last Saturday. He looked enough like Edith, he could have been her grandson." The elderly woman smiled at the memory but the smile disappeared when I asked my next question.

"Mrs. Beatty, would you be willing to testify in court that the person you saw enter the Semple house the afternoon of Stuart Goodenough's murder was Danny Danger?" I'd deliberately used the musician's stage name to see if that would cause her any confusion. "Bid . . . Bridget told the police that the person you both saw was Amanda Little."

"I would not hesitate in the least, my dear. He can change his last name but not his face. I know who I saw. When it comes to eyesight, I still don't need glasses unlike Bridget, who is so nearsighted that unless she has her glasses on or contacts in, she can't see her hand in front of her face. She wasn't wearing her glasses or contact lenses when we were looking out the window and for the record, my memory is as good as my eyesight. You can check that out with Doc Parker."

"If what you say is true, then why in the world would Bridget insist that you're wrong and she's right."

Vilma Beatty hesitated a moment before answering. "I think I can trust you as much as I believe you trust me and you will not repeat what I'm about to tell you," she said, looking me straight in the eye. "My daughter has many wonderful qualities and only one fault. She's a gossip. True, she did see someone but by the time she processed the foggy image through her brain, that someone became Amanda Little. And Amanda Little, in Bridget's circle of friends, makes a much better subject to gossip about than a person that they don't know, don't care to know, and doesn't live in this town."

Taking a deep breath and exhaling slowly, Vilma Beatty asked if I cared for a dram of sherry. "That young doctor, Doc Parker's nephew, I believe his name is Peter, recommended that I have one once in a while. He said it would be good for my legs," she said, pulling up the edge of the modest, cotton housecoat, revealing stick-thin legs clad in white support hose.

It was then that I noticed the red, felt slippers on her tiny feet. They were the kind of slippers that were made more for show than for walking.

From where I was sitting, I could reach out and touch the side table upon which sat the silver tray with the bottle of sherry and two crystal glasses. I was about to offer to pour a small amount of liquid into a glass and serve it to her when, to my surprise, Vilma got up from the settee. Taking a moment to get her balance, she hobbled over to the table and did the honors.

"That's another thing that you're going to have to keep to yourself, my dear," admonished Vilma with a wink. "If Bridget knew I've been practicing walking, she might tell that son-in-law of mine and he'd probably take my scooter back to the store for a refund." Steadying herself by placing her hand on my shoulder, Vilma then pushed off and made it back to the settee under her own power.

"Mrs. Beatty, would if be all right with you if I took a quick trip over to the Semple house? It'll only take a few minutes. There's something I need to check out." I didn't see any reason to explain to her that I wanted to assure myself that the painting I'd secretly named *A Study in Yellow* and the portrait entitled *Ethereal in Ecru* were one in the same. I also wanted to check the five frames in the cellar to see if and/or how they were connected to the Sisters series. "In fact, if you don't mind, I'll leave my purse here and just take my key and flashlight," I said, plunging my hand into the depths of the large leather bag and managing to snag both items on the first try, a true case of pure luck.

"I knew when you started asking me questions," said Vilma Beatty, her eyes bright with excitement, "that you were doing your detective thing and now you're going next door to do some more sleuthing. How would you like it if I hopped on my scooter and tagged along?"

"I'd consider it an honor but I don't think Bridget would approve. Besides," I said, pointing at the sherry bottle, "you know as well as I do, if you drink, you shouldn't drive."

"You're so right and that's why you're my designated driver." Vilma Beatty delivered the line with a straight face.

"Maybe next time," I replied before giving her a hug and reassuring her again, that I wouldn't be gone long.

Chapter thirty-five

✁

The Semple Victorian, in spite of the sunshine that was streaming through the uncovered windows, seemed to be cloaked in shadows. Not wanting to spend one minute longer than necessary in the old house, I walked directly to the cellar door, opened it, and before stepping inside, turned on the flashlight. As I expected, when I pulled the string to turn on the room's only source of light, nothing happened. The lightbulb had burned out. Throwing the flashlight's beam directly on the five empty picture frames that I'd earlier dismissed as being as uninteresting as they were empty, I turned them over, one by one. On the back of each frame was the name of its former occupant, beginning with the first portrait, *Lovely in Lilac* and ending with the fifth portrait, *Posed in Purple*.

Stepping out of the cellar, I switched off the flashlight and walked into the living room area to say good-bye to the melancholy, beautiful young woman depicted in the last of the Six Sisters series—Edith Semple, who indeed was ethereal in ecru.

Filled with emotional satisfaction, I spoke out loud and

addressed the subject by her name and told her how sorry I was that the closest she came to being his bride was to have her portrait painted by her beloved, Calvin Bean, aka Cabe.

"I don't exactly know what's going to happen to you once I go to my son-in-law with the circumstantial evidence I've gathered, but I hope you end up someplace that appreciates your sharing Calvin's talent with the outside world," I said. I chalked up the feeling that I wasn't alone as the result of my little farewell speech to Edith's image. "Well, so long, Edith, it's been interesting, no, make that enlightening, getting to know the real you."

"Why tell it to a picture when you can say it to her face?" came the raspy voice behind me.

Spinning quickly around, I expected to come face-to-face with Mrs. Daggert. Instead, I found myself standing toe-to-toe with someone whose image I'd seen on television ads trumpeting his upcoming concert in Indianapolis.

"Danny Semp . . . I mean Danger! How did you get in here?" I gasped, my eyes making the quick trip from his almost delicate face to the shiny black pistol clutched in his right hand.

"Hey, that's no fair," said the slim, slightly built young man with soft gray eyes and a long blond ponytail. "You know my name but I don't know yours. Why don't you introduce yourself before I blow your brains out," he informed me nonchalantly. "In answer to your question, I came in through the French doors that lead out to the side yard. A flick of a credit card and it was open-sesame time. Too bad for you that the flip was done with an eye on a fast profit, otherwise a double bolt lock and an alarm system might have saved your life." He paused and, using his left hand, shook a cigarette out of a nearly empty pack and lit it with a small, gold lighter.

Stuffing the pack and the lighter in the front pocket of his jeans, Danny Danger took a deep drag on the cigarette and coughed. "Bad habit. One of these days I'm going to quit. Now, where were we? Oh yeah, I remember. It's my turn to ask the questions. What's the name and what's your game?"

I found it difficult to answer with my mouth bone dry and my brain on hold. Somehow, I managed to croak out my name and inform him that my game was interior design. While he digested the information, I also managed to take my eyes off his hand long enough to get a good look at the popular heavy metal rocker.

With his long blond hair, fine-boned, long face devoid of theatrical makeup, and soft, light eyes, Danny did indeed bear a strong resemblance to the girl in the portrait above the fireplace—*Ethereal in Ecru*. Dressed in tight-fitting, white designer jeans and a mustard-colored, loose-fitting silk shirt, the slightly built Danny could easily be mistaken for a young woman, especially by the myopic Biddy McFarland.

Because I'd done a pretty good job keeping a low profile while conducting my own investigation, steering clear of Matt and the Castle Hills police, I had no hope of being rescued by the boys in blue. If I were going to get out of this alive, it would take more than logic, intuition, and luck. It would take divine intervention that often works in mysterious ways and sometimes with an outcome that is equally mysterious. I had a fleeting vision of my family and friends throwing roses on my grave, consoling one another with platitudes such as it was my time to go or at least I didn't suffer.

Perhaps if I was holding something in my hand more lethal than a standard household flashlight, I might have considered making a break for it. Instead, I stood there waiting for my captor, a double murderer, to make his move. Hoping to forestall the inevitable, I brought up the fact that should he pull the trigger, the noise would surely alert the next-door neighbors, the McFarlands, that something bad was happening at the Semple house.

"Not hardly." Danny sniggered. "The owners are almost never home during the day and the only other person in the house is a crippled old lady who lives upstairs. Hardly a threat, wouldn't you agree? Besides, I plan on doing the deed in the cellar. I don't want to take a chance of getting any blood splatter on the portrait. Something like that might detract from its value and I imagine I'd have to explain how the splatter got there to whoever I hire to clean it."

With nothing to lose but my life (something that seemed to be a given at this point), I asked my captor what the connection was between himself, Stuart Goodenough, Bambi Eastwood, and the painting. It was more to satisfy my curiosity than a stalling tactic since I'd resigned myself to the fact that barring a miracle, the vision I'd had of the graveside farewell was in the offing and sooner rather than later.

Flicking the half-smoked cigarette into the fireplace, the rocker took a minute to consider my question. "I first ran into the 'dynamic duo' when I was playing in some of the, shall we say, less-than-five-star lounges in Vegas. I believe it was in Pussy Sweet's Gentlemen's Club, a real dive. Bambi was the star attraction, and for want of a better word, Stuart was her pimp. When the two of them weren't fleecing the customers, they were dreaming up new con games."

I waited while Danny lit another cigarette and for the coughing that followed to subside. Perhaps it was pure fear that had taken hold of my senses because given the situation I was in, a cigarette was the last thing I wanted before going to meet my maker. I felt absolution for all my sins was the wiser and better choice than a nicotine fix.

"I lost track of them around the time they divorced the second time," he continued. "By then I had a new agent and was headlining at all the big hotels and casinos on the strip. I was raking in more money than I knew what to do with and ended up putting most of it up my nose." Shaking his head at the memory, Danny took a deep drag on the cigarette.

When he picked up the story again, the smoke that

hadn't reached his lungs slowly escaped through his nose and mouth. "It was when I hit bottom that I started seeing a shrink on a regular basis. He told me my problem was that I have an addictive personality. He said I should channel it in a healthier direction and suggested that I start collecting art. Man, before I knew it, I'm hanging out at auction houses, art galleries, and rubbing shoulders with all the big shots in the art world. As private collections go," Danny bragged, "mine is one of the finest. It cost me most of what was left of my money but like I told my agent and my manager, I'm worth it."

"And as you were saying about Stuart and Bambi . . ." I prompted. At least, I said to myself, before I die, I'll have answers to a lot of the things that my investigation didn't uncover.

Danny ignored my effort to move the conversation in another direction. "As I was saying, I was in a real cash-flow crunch when some old lady that I didn't even know existed dies and leaves me a fortune in dough along with a dilapidated old house filled with junk. Being the star that I am, my windfall made the network news along with the fact that I now had enough money to purchase the one picture every collector in the world coveted, the missing Sixth Sister portrait."

"So you got ahold of Stuart and sold him the house," I said, making a second attempt to change directions.

"It wasn't quite like that," he said, looking at me like I wasn't the sharpest pin in the cushion. "Actually, I sent my agent to check out the house and its contents. He came back with the advice to sell the old dump and everything in it to the first fool to come along."

"And that was Stuart Goodenough and the Fast Flippers," I said, believing that I had gotten through to him and could die happy. Well, maybe not happy but at least knowing I did the best I could. Too bad, I thought to myself, this part wouldn't be in my investigative report, the one I hoped would make its way to Matt after I was gone.

"Yeah. Sneaky Stuart rounded up a small group of

suckers and sold them on the idea of making a fast profit on the fast flip of this old place. When I found out him and his group bought the house, I thought I'd put one over on the bastard until I found out that I was the one who got shafted in the deal," said Danny, losing the battle to suppress his hacking cough.

Having no other choice, I waited until he stopped coughing. While I waited, I tried to think of some way I could get out of the dilemma I was in and came up empty. I had to bite my tongue not to remind my captor that nobody forced him to sell the house and its contents to Stuart's Fast Flippers.

"I guess when Stuart discovered the last of the Six Sisters portraits, *Ethereal in Ecru*, in the house and the five empty frames in the cellar," said Danny when he was finally able to speak, "he put two and two together and came up with a way to get his paws on a whole lot of my moolah. He actually thought that I was stupid enough to pay money to get back what should've been mine in the first place. Ain't that the dumbest thing you ever heard?"

Not knowing what else to do or say, I nodded my head and once again waited until he stopped coughing long enough to continue, which, after what seemed like an eternity, he finally did.

"We even had a drink on the deal from the bottle of booze I'd brought along. That's when I slipped the stuff in his drink. I took the bottle and the glasses with me when I left but I forgot to take his keys. That's why I had to get Bambi involved. I figured she'd have a key to his penthouse and I needed to get in there 'cause that's where Stuart said he stashed the painting. Can you imagine," cried Danny, his voice filled with indignation, "here the guy's dying and he lies to me. I hate liars, don't you? I shoulda figured with him being a con man that he would do something sneaky like hiding the portrait in plain sight. It finally dawned on me that's what he did."

I couldn't help but think how different things would have been if only Danny had hired a reputable appraiser to check out the house and its contents instead of giving that job to his theatrical agent. Although he explained why he killed Stuart, I had to ask him why he killed Bambi. The question seemed to make him uncomfortable.

"Man, she was a real loony tune. Once we got in the penthouse, she starts doing her old Vegas act and saying how wonderful it was going to be when the two of us were on stage together. That's when I knew that I had to get rid of her. I have enough troubles getting my act past the censors without adding total nudity and dirty dancing to it," said Danny, sounding more like a prig than the bad boy of heavy metal rockers. "I thought it was kinda apropos that I used the same stuff on Bambi that her and Stu used on her Vegas customers. Her death was neater than Stuart's. I didn't give him enough in his drink, that's why I had to smother him."

"Speaking of Stuart's death," I said trying to sound normal in an abnormal situation, "how and why did Amanda Little's key and chain end up in the window seat with his body?"

"Oh that," he said, shrugging his thin shoulders, "was nothing more than an afterthought. I found them earlier when I was in the side yard. I didn't know or care who they belonged to so I tossed them in with the body. I thought it was a nice touch. A bit theatrical, but nice. Actually, I think the suicide confession note on the computer was better. The cops in Castle Hills are almost as dumb as the ones in Seville."

"While we're on the subject of Castle Hills, weren't you worried that the doorman could identify you as the last person in and out of the penthouse?" I asked, ignoring the old saw regarding curiosity and a dead cat. If I was going to die (and trust me, I thought I was), I wanted to go knowing I'd collected all the pieces of the puzzle and put them in their places.

"Nah. Bambi had already let it slip that he's only on duty from eight at night to six in the morning. So much for security. For the money places like that charge, you'd think that they'd at least install some cameras but they didn't.

"Enough with the talking," he said in an eerily even tone. "No GHB, no pillows. Only a well-aimed bullet and blam! Show's over, at least for you. Too bad you won't be around to see me make my exit with the last of the Six Sisters tucked under my arm. I'll miss your applause. Come on, it's showtime."

With the weapon pressed against the back of my neck, I began to shuffle toward the cellar still clutching the flashlight in my hand. As we passed the dining room area, I thought I heard a familiar sound. Unfortunately, almost as soon as I identified it, the sound was gone.

"What was that?" Danny demanded, stopping to listen. He'd wrapped his left arm around my waist so I couldn't wander away while he tried to identify something that he wasn't even sure he'd heard.

"Maybe it was a ghost," I said, hoping to rattle him into loosening his grip on me, something that might've given me at least a chance to make a break for it. I'd decided that if it was my time to go, I wasn't going to make it easy for either one of us. I remembered reading about people literally being scared to death so I repeated the comment, aware that my captor had a reputation for being terrified of ghosts.

"No way," retorted Danny, "I poured salt all around the foundation. Take it from me, it works. I did that last Saturday afternoon and to be on the safe side, I did it again today. Whatever it was, it's gone now."

I knew that the sound I'd heard was Vilma's scooter. The elderly woman most likely was worried when I hadn't returned as promised and had made an attempt to find me only to discover that unlike the McFarland house, the Semple place was not handicapped accessible. I went directly to the top with my silent prayer that Vilma had made it safely back to her second-floor sitting room.

We'd resumed our trek to the cellar when the unmistakable sound of the French doors crashing open filled the house. Both Danny and I reacted to the noise. Like dance partners, we stepped away from one another and faced our audience, which in this case was an audience of one—Vilma Beatty.

With her voice as steady as the two hands that were holding the biggest gun I'd ever seen, she ordered Danny to put down his weapon. His immediate reaction was to point it directly at Vilma's frail body. Moving quicker than I thought possible, I slammed his wrist with my flashlight, causing him to drop the black pistol.

He made a dive for the skidding weapon and was about to pick it up when Vilma stopped him in his tracks. "Don't be a fool, Danny. We both know that at this range, if I pull the trigger I won't miss."

Although she didn't sound like Clint Eastwood when he delivered a similar line in *Dirty Harry*, the weapon she was holding was an exact match to the one that was used in the movie, except Vilma's wasn't a prop. It was a for real Smith & Wesson model 29, commonly known as a .44 Magnum.

If Vilma didn't intimidate Danny, the weapon certainly did. He didn't move so much as an eyelash when I picked up the black pistol along with my flashlight and moved over to where Vilma was standing. I didn't know how long the strength in her legs would last and thought it would be a good idea to be her backup.

Vilma was in the middle of telling me that the gun, which she kept in her knitting bag, was a gift she'd given to her husband on their tenth wedding anniversary when the ear-piecing scream of a police siren interrupted her story.

"Oh, thank heavens. For a while there, I was afraid that Jasper Merkle thought I was a dotty old lady when I phoned the station and told him that we needed help with the flip-house murderer."

We watched as Officer Patti Crump clamped the cuffs on the double murderer before putting him in the police car for the short ride to jail. When the police vehicle disappeared from sight, I escorted Vilma to where she'd parked her scooter in the side yard of the property. I was hesitant about returning the weapon to the knitting bag that dangled from the scooter's handle and said as much to Vilma.

"Why on earth not?" she wanted to know before adding, "the thing isn't even loaded. Now, let's get me back to my sitting room before Bridget comes home. I think we could both use a dram of sherry. Doctor's orders, you know."

"You got that right, partner," I replied. "And if we hurry, I might even beat Charlie home." And I did.

Epilogue

Danny Semple, aka Danny Danger, was charged with two counts of first-degree murder in the deaths of Stuart Good-enough and Bambi Eastwood. His high-priced lawyer advised him to enter a guilty plea rather than face the ultimate punishment—the death penalty. The heavy metal rocker went for it faster than his career went down the drain. He ended up with two life sentences without the possibility of parole. The only thing left unsettled was the ownership of the last, and possibly the best, of Calvin Bean's work, *Ethereal in Ecru*, and it was one puzzle that I'm glad I didn't have to solve. And that's no lie.

Instead of the usual lecture from Matt and Charlie about my being a designer and not a detective, Matt actually thanked me for the circumstantial evidence I'd collected and turned over to him. In turn, Charlie expressed his forgiveness for my sleuthing by taking me to Chicago for a weekend getaway where we stayed at a delightful, small hotel just off Michigan Avenue and within walking distance to Water Tower Place, the ultimate place to shop in the Windy City.

Harry Eastwood paid all the monies due Duke Demarco and Designer Jeans. The Cosgroves roared back
into town on their Harleys, took one look at the Semple
house and bought it the same day that they sold their old
house, the "retro" ranch, to Harry Eastwood. Harry recon-
ciled with his first wife, Helen, who Mary insists is a dead
ringer for Florence Henderson.

With her reputation restored (Hilly Murrow made a
public apology of sorts, writing a column on the risk of
unisex apparel) Amanda Little wed Arthur Kraft in a private ceremony. The couple honeymooned in Arthur's Castle Hills condo.

Before starting the Eastwood project (a modest updat-
ing of the interior of the ranch house) Designer Jeans did a
partial makeover of Vilma Beatty's sitting room. With
some input from Biddy, JR and I managed to make a col-
lage of old photos, posters, and other World War II memorabilia that Vilma had saved from her stint as a navy nurse.
She was both surprised and pleased with the results. And
Gordy McFarland was pleased that the partial makeover
was done free of charge. I felt that it was the least I could
do for a brave lady who truly had risked life and limb to
come to my rescue.

In recognition for their help in my investigation into the
two murders, I babysat Kris and the twins while JR and
Mary enjoyed a day trip to Springvale that included two
tickets for the Springvale Film Festival. This was a real
sacrifice on my part since the festival included a showing
of classic films from the forties and fifties. Like I said to
JR when I handed her the tickets, "Here's looking at you
kid."

A HELPING HAND
FOR A PAINTED LADY

(Or How to Live with and in an Old Victorian Manse)

The reason I went with the above title is that I grew up in such a house. After many years and moves, my parents returned to the neighborhood that my mother called home. She had fond memories of tree-lined streets, shady sidewalks and houses with porches big enough to accommodate the adults and children who gathered there after the evening meal to watch the world go by. When my parents came home to where we were living at the time—a small house with two bedrooms and one bath, hardly suitable for a family of four girls and one boy—and announced that they had purchased a Victorian in Mother's old neighborhood, we kids were sure that we were moving into a palace.

According to my mother, the house was so large that each child could have their own room. It also had a winding stairway leading to the upper floor and two full bathrooms. "I remember passing the house every day on my way to school," Mother had said, "and even then it was considered to be one of the oldest and grandest houses in the neighborhood." Surely, we were on our way to living the American Dream. Little did we suspect that we would be living out that dream in a nightmare of a house.

The first time I saw the house, even though I was only five at the time, I realized that Mother was seeing everything I did but through rose-colored glasses. The old house's Victorian architecture, inside and out, had been all but destroyed by previous attempts to transform the place from out-of-date to up-to-date. My parents had purchased an authentic money pit.

To give you a small taste of what my parents had to deal with and eventually overcome, I've complied a short list of some of the more memorable things:

No central heat
A partially excavated basement
No storm doors, screens, or gutters
Doors that wouldn't open and windows that wouldn't close
A maze of odd-shaped rooms
One miniscule-size closet in the entire house
A long, dangerously narrow, squeaky staircase
Plaster walls in dire need of repair
A severe shortage of electric outlets
Layer upon layer of wallpaper and paint

The old house had so many crazy quirks that you had to either laugh or cry. We kids laughed while Mom and Dad cried as they tried to keep up with the constant need for home repairs.

So my advice to all you would-be owners of a painted lady is to be sure the lady is in good enough condition to survive a facelift or a flip. Remember, sometimes such changes can be fatal.

DECORATING TIPS THAT SELL

When selling your house, its decor is often appreciated by the homeowner, dismissed by the real estate agent (he or she is more often concerned, and rightly so, with things such as the heating and cooling system, obvious needed repairs such as peeling paint and ceiling stains, and curb appeal), and ignored by the prospective buyer. So take a minute and consider my suggestions; they may help you sell your house faster and for more money. If nothing else, you might enjoy the new look and decide to stay put for a while longer until the market improves.

Paint all the rooms in light, neutral colors such as beige, pale green, creamy yellow, or ivory. This allows the prospective buyer to imagine their own furniture in the rooms without thinking that their magenta-colored sofa or turquoise bedspread would look awful in the room.

Remove everything that isn't nailed down from the top of every surface in your home and place items in a storage box. Then, once you have cleaned and polished the various surfaces, go back into each room with the box and return only the necessary items. Nothing says lack of storage more than a bunch of knickknacks or appliances on a countertop.

If you have a pet, keep it and its dishes, bowls, bedding, and toys out of sight while you or your agent is showing your home. Same advice if you have a smoker in your home; keep ashtrays and smoking accessories out of sight and open the windows for fresh air.

If you have small children, let them pick out a couple of toys, books, and the like and store the rest until your house is sold. You would be surprised how well your kids can get along without a room overflowing with toys.

Don't bake a fresh batch of cookies. That once was a great tip but so many people followed it that now it's almost like hanging a sign on the front door that there is something about your house that you're trying to hide. Instead, soak a little piece of cotton in vanilla and place it behind a cup or stack of dishes in your kitchen cabinet. It has the same effect as the cookie baking but it's not so obvious.

Buyers seem to have developed a thing for closet space. Don't lose a sale because of a stuffed closet. Do yourself and those less fortunate a favor and clean out your closet. Donate the usable items to your favorite charity and bring the rest to a recycle center. While you're at it, do the same with your kids' toy box, dresser drawers, and closets. Centers for abused women and homeless shelters are always interested in usable items and clothing.

Nothing says you care more than a clean house and that includes, walls, floors, windows, and bedding. Don't blow selling your house because of laziness. The most lovely or expensive decor won't help your house show off its best features when they are hidden by dust, dirt, clutter, and bad odors.

Last but not least, keep in mind that potential buyers have come to visit your house and not you. Allow it to speak for itself beginning with a newly purchased mat that says WELCOME.

Penguin Group (USA) Online

What will you be reading tomorrow?

Tom Clancy, Patricia Cornwell, W.E.B. Griffin,
Nora Roberts, William Gibson, Robin Cook,
Brian Jacques, Catherine Coulter, Stephen King,
Dean Koontz, Ken Follett, Clive Cussler,
Eric Jerome Dickey, John Sandford,
Terry McMillan, Sue Monk Kidd, Amy Tan,
John Berendt…

You'll find them all at
penguin.com

Read excerpts and newsletters,
find tour schedules and reading group guides,
and enter contests.

Subscribe to Penguin Group (USA) newsletters
and get an exclusive inside look
at exciting new titles and the authors you love
long before everyone else does.

PENGUIN GROUP (USA)
us.penguingroup.com